BREAKING NORMS

(A Story of Love, Agony and Tolerance)

By

Mita Balani

MITA BALANI

Published in USA by Pixie Dust LLC, 2017

EBook ISBN: 978-0-9986033-0-8

Paperback ISBN: 978-0-9986033-1-5

CONTENTS

CHAPTER 1. SEE HER AGAIN

May 2012
New Jersey
Present Day

I DRAG RAJEEV TO THE MALL for shopping on a Sunday afternoon. Otherwise, he never cares to take me out. There is a shopping mall close to our apartment in New Jersey. But this is only the second time I have been to the mall in the eleven and a half months since we got married.

Rajeev is a workaholic geek. He can spend hours sitting in front of a computer, talking to the screen and resolving his work problems, but he never likes to shop, especially with me. He is passionate about his work and tends to prioritize professional life over any other aspect of his life. He brings his laptop to bed almost every night. That upsets me. It doesn't help nurture our already disjointed relationship. Since we got married, not even once have we watched a movie together. There is no sign of romance between us. They say for married couples, some of the most important, intimate conversations take place in their bedroom during the fading hours of the day. But this certainly is not true for us since Rajeev converses with his office software program during those hours. I have tried starting conversations many times, but he shuts it off by simply saying, "I need to finish this first. Can we talk later?" But later never comes. There are many other things I could report.

I enjoy being at the mall. The dry scent of perfumes screaming out loud from the counters of various shops, new clothes smell, and clean, shiny floors—all of it attracts me to shopping. It makes me feel good in a strange way.

I step into a few shops one after another, and he follows me silently. I browse through the clearance section of each of those shops to check if I like anything. I have been looking around for an hour to no avail. What I like is expensive and what is not expensive is not appealing. Frustrated, Rajeev steps out of Macy's store. I follow him out quietly. He insists to go to the food court instead of shopping any more. I see signs of a bad mood spiraling over him, especially since I could not buy anything in the last hour. His eyes turn red. He won't think twice before creating a scene even in a public place. I smother my urge to dig into more clearance racks. We make our way to the food court.

On our way, I see many stores that grab my attention and tempt me to shop or at least look around. But I don't stop because I am scared that he might get mad.

His loud shriek still echoes in my ears every time we go out. Unlike other times, once he accompanied me to a nearby supermarket for grocery shopping. I spotted frozen packets of palak paneer and dal makhani placed next to piles of buffalo wings and chicken burrito packets. It was exciting to see this supermarket finally carrying Indian food. I just stood there staring at those packets, with my eyes brimming with a yearning to buy it. I imagined my eyes looking at them the way a small kid looks at the ice cream that mom won't buy him. When Rajeev realized that I was not following him, he turned back to look for me. He squealed loud enough to turn heads, "What the heck are you staring at? Can't you just keep walking behind me without making any extra stop? Let's go." His scream left me startled. I was embarrassed and sad. All the people shopping around there gaped at us. Few whispered something to their partners; I don't know for sure but it felt like they were talking about us. After that I kept strolling behind him as fast as I could with my eyes fixated on the ground to avoid eye contact with anyone in the crowd who heard his screaming.

I will never repeat that kind of episode. So I just follow him to the food court quietly. We were passing by the kids play area and I see her.

I can't believe what I see, as if I am dreaming. Never in my unconscious had I imagined that we would run into each other again in this life; that too at a place far from where we left our past. Unknowingly, my feet freeze there. My body feels too heavy to move forward. In the kids play area, she is helping a cute little boy take his shoes off. She is tending this kid with her full attention. She doesn't notice me at first. I stand still looking at her. Within seconds, she looks up after sending two kids off to play, a toddler boy and a girl—who seems around four years old. Suddenly, a flood of happiness runs through my heart. I didn't see it coming. My eyes brim with joyful tears.

Esha is almost in tears too when she sees me. Her lips quiver as water jumps out of her eyes. I can barely smile. Neither of us hugs the other, nor do we speak. It is an awkward moment for both of us. We don't know how to react. This very instance brings to life several questions that have long been dead for me. Questions, for a long time now, for which I wanted to claim an answer from her. Our eyes—imbued with pain, love, and a tiny hint of anger—meet. Those curious sets of eyeballs barely smile at each other, then query each other and immediately move on without even waiting for answers.

Quickly, I run behind Rajeev to catch up with him. Halfway through the food court, I turn around and look at Esha one more time. I feel dreadful about not being able to speak to her. I move forward swimming through the flood of emotions. She still looks as beautiful as she looked eight years ago except her big almond-shaped eyes appear vapid now.

This mall doesn't offer that many food choices. We end up picking spinach Alfredo pizza. I sprinkle crushed red chilies on it. When I am about to take the first bite of pizza, I notice Esha coming in my direction to the food court. This is the first time I am thankful for Rajeev's resistance to shopping. His bad mood is keeping his eyes fixed on the pizza slice. He doesn't see Esha coming; not that he knows her. With my mouth still open, my hand holding a piece of pizza, my eyes gaze at her. My heart skips a beat when she approaches our table. Coming closer at a hand's distance, she stares at me too. We are at a distance where I could hear what she says or she could overhear what I might say. Our eyes gawk at each other again, a little more intense this time as if we both are enticed to speak, but a little hesitant, too.

Her son is crying because Mom Esha is lost in her thoughts to pay attention to what the little one is saying. Her daughter is being a nice elder sister, trying to calm him while shaking mommy to bring her back to this world. "Mom . . . Mom. What are you thinking?" she yells. Then she expresses in a cute way, "Big sister, Gauri, and little brother Harsh are right here, by you. Let's go home."

The way her daughter looks and talks is an exact copy of Esha. I still remember her childhood pictures I had seen in her room.

As much as I want to talk to her, I am too scared to exchange a word for Rajeev might come to know about us. I am also petrified by the thought of her leaving me one more time. In spite of all the thoughts and frights that are crowding my head, I stand up to move in her direction. I don't want to lose a chance to yell at her, scream at her and get the answers to my questions. I want to tell her how mad I have been at her all this while. All of a sudden, I want everything to go back to normal between us. The invisible wall of hesitation that is standing strong separating us, I want to break that wall. But the next thought brings heaviness in my legs. I can't take a single step further. The fact that she is married and has two kids stops me from questioning her.

Maybe I don't care for her as much as before, I lie to myself to reduce my anger, to calm my anxiety. *After all, why should I care for her now? She left me, I didn't leave her.* I blame her to hide my emotions. One more time I fail to stand up for myself. One more time I give in to circumstances instead of chasing what I want, what I wish in life. It is partly my submissiveness and partly the fear of losing her one more time and getting hurt to not heal ever again. I choose to be quiet. She grabs both of her kids hands and walks right out of the mall, maybe to go home.

After my encounter with Esha in the mall on Sunday, I leave the awkward moment behind. Cutting through the shoppers' crowd, I walk out with Rajeev, as if, one more time, leaving behind all those questions I have for her. Maybe I have accepted that our paths are now different. But little did I understand then that, in the back of my mind, I was still thinking about her and about our best time together. Secretly, my mind desires to make a present and future of that wonderful past.

*****

Monday Morning

After Rajeev leaves for the office, I finish the everyday chores and sit on the sofa to watch TV. Lost in my own thoughts, I press TV remote buttons like crazy and stare at the screen blankly still thinking about Esha. I am unable to take her out of my thoughts. This upsets me even more than actually seeing her. While flipping through channels, the news on one catches my attention.

"Five people (including two teenagers, an immigrant Indian mother and her two kids) were hospitalized after a three-vehicle accident yesterday evening on Highway I-78 near Center Point Mall, local officials said."

Jitters run through me when I think, *Could it be Esha?* An immigrant Indian mother with two kids and near Center Point Mall? And that too, yesterday; this feels ominous.

I fix my eyes and ears on the TV.

"Two vehicles were trying to merge at the intersection. They both collided with a third vehicle causing all traffic to stand still." the news continued.

"John A. Davis, the nineteen-year-old driver of one vehicle, and his sixteen-year-old passenger and his sister, April A. Davis, were injured and taken to a nearby hospital. Thirty-eight-year-old Indian mother Priya Pande and her two children were injured and taken to a nearby hospital as well. The fifty-year-old driver of the third car lost the battle for his life at the site of the accident."

I am sad for the people who got in this brutal accident. But I also heave a sigh of relief knowing it is not Esha.

"Police said they're still investigating the crash."

I tell myself *I don't care for her anymore. I am only angry at her.* Perhaps, it seems, I have mastered the art of burying the past somewhere inside me till it finds its way up in the present.

"Hell yeah girl, I still care about you," I speak out loud. Turning off the TV and angrily tossing the remote control on the sofa, I cry.

My crying goes from sobbing to loud crying. I feel helpless that I still care about her, but can't be with her. I always thought sadness would fly away, riding on wings of time. But I was wrong. With time, sadness is bubbling up and up. I cry some more, crimping up in a corner of the sofa. Tears make my vision and thinking blurry. Once again, my heart is racing in fury to gain answers to all the questions I have for her. Why couldn't she break the promise she gave to her dad? Why didn't she try to fulfill the assurances she gave me? The care, the concern for Esha and the questions that are blooming afresh again in front of me, drive my mind back to the time, when I met her and dwelled in bountiful happiness, which was all blown away in the blink of an eye.

CHAPTER 2. FIRST WARNING

January 2003
Mumbai

WHEN YOU HAVE JUST TURNED eighteen and you dream about the love of your life, hardly anyone takes you seriously. They think you are crazy and wild. On top of that, Girish drops a *Human Anatomy* book in my lap and lashes out, "Are you crazy or what? You seriously need to read this book. It will help you understand stuff, some differences between a man and a woman," and walks away.

Girish—a tall, handsome Mona Punjabi guy— down to earth and sorted. My cousin brother, my uncle's— my dad's brother's—son, my best buddy. His eyeglasses—rectangular plastic frames with black as the prominent color and a hint of red used to form a mosaic pattern—makes him look somber and serious. But that is totally deceiving of his lighthearted and cheerful personality.

Our families live in Neelam Nagar, Phase 2, Mulund East, Mumbai. Our parents believe in simple living, unlike the flamboyant lifestyle that most of our relatives prefer. Our flats are next to each other. We are always at his place studying, eating, gossiping, wrestling, and getting into mischief. Girish is the only child of his parents, but not spoiled at all. My elder sister is more spoiled. We are a family of four, my mom, dad, and not to forget an elder sister—she used to live with us. Now she is married and lives with her husband. Girish and I call her Di—elder sister. Di and I are two opposite ends of the same pole that are never meant to get along well unless a miracle happens. As a result, I rarely stay home—when Di is around—as much as I stay at Girish's place.

Di has always been jealous of a friendship Girish and I share. She doesn't share that special relationship with any of our cousins. No one else but she herself is responsible for that. She always lives on cloud nine, in her own world. She is a self-obsessed girl whose world revolves around her own self. On the other hand, I have always been considerate, polite, submissive, and concerned about other people's happiness. Even though my height of five feet three is above average for an Indian female, my plump body always makes me self-conscious. On top of that, the degree to which nosey relatives make a big deal about my few extra pounds doesn't help at all. This is why I never dare to experiment with different dressing styles. I am always happy in my simple jeans and t-shirt, with my hair tied up in a high pony tail. Many people say I have a beautiful smile. So I always wear it with the canine teeth peeping gently out of my smile. Di on the other hand likes everything perfecto from head to toe.

She never misses a chance to boss me around. I sometimes wonder how I have survived in the same room with her for these many years. Many times her annoying habits make me angry. A peace-loving person like me can't even understand why she acts the way she does. The undeniable fact to be told, she oversteps every boundary around her. She tries to control and manipulate everyone surrounding her, either directly—as in my case or using tricks—as in our parents' case.

I don't have my own friends either. I always hang out with Girish's friends. Maybe hanging out with those boys has contributed to my already existing unruffled attitude. But sometimes I wish I could have learned from them how to be emotionally stronger and not give in easily. Being docile breaks my heart many times in a million ways, hurts me again and again. His friends are my friends. His friends were my friends till he went to medical college; I was in eleventh grade then. Girish is two years elder to me. He wants to be a cardiologist. It has been almost two years now since Girish and all our friends have graduated from high school. I am the lonely person in that school now without my hangout gang. Always being with Girish and his gang, I never made my own friends, I never made my own decisions, and I just tagged along with him for everything. At school, Girish protected me and at home Di always bossed me around. For so long in my life, I didn't even think about what I like and what I don't. I always did whatever made people around me happy. But now when once in a while I want to make my own choices, it's hard to stick to those choices and make my loved ones happy too all at the same time.

*****

January 2003
Two months before my twelfth exams
I complain to Girish that he hardly has time for me. Ever since he joined medical college, our schedules have been way different. He has been super swamped with college work. His typical day schedule is much busier than I could imagine. His alarm rings at seven every morning. After hitting snooze a few times, he gets out of bed at 7:15 AM. Breakfast, tea, squeeze in fifteen to twenty minutes of study time and then he leaves the house at eight to catch the local train to Nerul, where his college is. He builds in roughly twenty minutes of buffer time. A whole day of lectures, labs, and seminars during lunch time. He hits the gym for one hour before coming home. Finally he reaches home around 8:15 PM. 8:30 PM shower, 8:45 dinner, and then more studying. Sometimes he studies at home by himself.

Then other times he is group studying and comes home late. By the time he goes to bed, it is midnight. Besides, now he has new friends, a new purpose in life. We barely spend any time with each other. He has a holiday alternate Saturdays. At last, he promises to spend time with me one of these days.

*****

The following Saturday

I wave bye to my classmates and trail out of school towards the exit gate to go home. I am surprised and happy at the same time to see Girish there. He is sitting on the school katta—concrete bench just outside the main gate. I run to him and sit next to him on the katta to chat unlimited. Pointing to a hawker who is standing just outside the school gate, I ask, "Do you remember how we used to eat mouthwatering panipuri, sour ber, and imbli together, right here?"

"Hellooo . . . I never ate ber and imbli, only you ate it," his male ego interrupts my words. But soon he gets excited and we laugh our heads off when he reminds me, "The sourness of ber and imbli made you wink a zillion times . . . like this, see . . . see like this," he says, laced with the act of winking.

My instant reaction is to playfully smack him. But he is right. The first few times, my winking even gave wrong signals to the boys staring at me. But soon many were disappointed after understanding the real story about my winks.

He continues, "The best part of that time was sitting here to watch the beautiful girls of our school and talk about them."

During recess, we used to eat our lunch and play with the whole gang. But as soon as school was dismissed, the two of us always met outside the school's main gate. That was the unspoken protocol between us. We always sat on the katta and shared the whole day of classes in fifteen minutes. He would always tease me, "Look at that girl, she looks zhakas—sexy." I would always say, "Oh yeah, she sure does." I miss those fun-filled days.

One of my batch mates, Esha, is gorgeous and the most popular girl of the school. The gleam in her eyes is uncommonly attractive. It has a unique and mysterious charm that casts a spell on me every passing day. Everybody would die to talk to her; at least I would. In her navy blue chudidar and tight-fitting white short kurti, she looks amazingly pretty. She passes by the katta with her friends. A strand of hair touches her soft and smooth face skin. She gently tucks that hair strand behind her ear with her long and beautiful fingers. She doesn't notice us. She is not one of my acquaintances yet. But I would love to be friends with her.

I still remember when I saw her the first time—a tall and dusky girl with shoulder-length hair worn loose, laughing heartily with a sparkle in her almond-shaped brown eyes. She stood out amidst her group of friends. I had never seen such a vivacious person before. The vibrancy of her tone and her smile made my heart pound harder.

Girish, sitting next to me on my right-hand side, says, "Look at that girl, second from left; she is damn beautiful and sexy."

He makes me so angry that I want to hit him, right in his face. I can barely contain myself. I punch his right upper arm very hard.

"Ouch, that hurts," he screams.

I don't know where I got that much strength from. The passion for something can really make one strong.

He is surprised and raises his eyebrow. "What? Why are you mad?"

"Hey, you know how you always used to say to me . . . look at this girl, look at that girl . . . she is cute, she is sensuous. And I would reply, 'Oh yeah, she sure is'?" I say passionately.

A more intense look dominates my face. "I never said it to please you. I really meant it. With other girls it was fine, but Esha . . . she is mine, I l-i-k-e her. Better stay away from her."

My words take him to a world of rage, in a way I have never seen him before.

His eyes and face turn red. He storms out of there. Before leaving, he wails at the top of his lungs, "Are you crazy or what? Think before you say anything."

Completely scared, I follow him quietly. I avoid looking around because his shouting has set the eyes of the nearby street vendors on me. After walking a few steps he slows down and I stroll faster. Now we walk side by side without uttering a single word.

After a few minutes of silence, I gather the courage to say, "Listen, I have thought about it a lot before saying it. I have been pondering about it for quite a while now."

"You seriously need to read human anatomy books. That will help you understand some stuff," he scowls but says it without screaming.

Maybe because we are in the middle of the road, he maintains low volume in his voice. But I have never seen him this livid before. The rest of the way home is filled with an uncomfortable silence between us.

That evening Girish comes home. This time he looks calmer compared to the afternoon. A thought touches my mind, *we have been best buddies, so, maybe, he is trying to understand how I feel*. A little happy cloud dances over me. That happiness doesn't last long when he throws B. D. Chaurasia's human anatomy book in my lap and says, "Soni, we are boys, we like girls, that is absolutely normal and totally fine. You always hang out with me and my friends. You hardly have any friends that are girls, but that doesn't mean you should like—I mean love—girls like we boys do. Please—I am saying please—read this book and try to understand the anatomy of girls and boys. There is a difference." Then he finishes by sternly looking into my eyes and saying with a stony voice, "You get me?"

His new avatar leaves me startled and scared to death.

Not that I need to read B. D. Chaurasia to understand the difference between a man and a woman. I know it. Over the last few years, I have felt an intense attraction toward girls. And, Esha, I absolutely love her. Every time I see her, my heart flutters like a butterfly who just came out of the chrysalis and whose wings are still not dry enough to fly. But it can't control itself. The same way. The exact same way, my heart dances, flaps every single time I get a glimpse of her. I love Esha. Many times, I have dreamt about her with open eyes. Not only that, a few months back, I also scribbled few lines while daydreaming about her, something that I have never done before in my life.

Your bright smile creates havoc in me.

The liveliness of your laugh touches my heart to the deepest.

Appearing in my dreams, day and night,

The sweet, emotional pain that you have given

me is beyond tolerance now.

I desire to spend life holding you in my arms.

I wish to relieve life being in your arms.

Only the feeling of love could bring those words out of me.

"But Girish . . ."

He doesn't let me finish the statement. "I don't want to hear any ifs or buts. Read the book. Remember, you are not a kid any more. Better think ten times before you say anything." And he walks away from there slamming the door behind, leaving me feeling guilty for loving someone dearly.

He says what I am feeling for her is not right. But I don't see it as wrong. I don't sleep a wink that night. The whole night, I think about what he said and how I feel. The whole night, I contend with my own thoughts. My own mind turns into my clever foe, leaving me miserable and unhappy, dropping me at the corner of a bifurcated road, for me to decide one path over the other to walk on.

*****

One week pass by. I can't choose one track over the other. Both are equally important. Girish is my closest person. He has always been. But, my other side—my heart falling for a girl. That is who I am. Can anyone change this part of me? Maybe not. I can't concentrate on studies even though final board exams are only months away. I continue struggling with my own thoughts. I even have doubted myself. *Is something, anything wrong with me?*

Girish has not talked to me at all for this week. He has been avoiding me.

Every time he ignores me, I regret the words I said to him that day in school. I want to slap myself for not keeping my mouth shut about her.

The way he ignores me is killing me. His silent treatment makes me sad and gloomy, reminding me of the hush of a country road at night. I always notice the dark pavement whenever I go for overnight road travel with my parents. This situation is similar; a bit scary too. His silence causes my mind to shrink into itself. My laugh ceases. Even though I consider nothing is wrong with me, I decide not to think about Esha again just because Girish means a world to me. I don't want to lose my best buddy at any cost.

On Saturday evening, I go to his house. Instead of entering his room directly, as I used to do till a week before, I make a stop in the living room.

I greet his parents. "Namaste, uncle. Namaste, aunty."

Aunty says, "Namaste, Beta—kiddo. What's the matter? You didn't enter Girish's room directly. He too seems upset for the last few days. What's going on? Did you guys fight again or what?"

"Nothing, aunty. I will go talk to him," I reply, pretending to be fine.

"Now you guys are getting older. Stop arguing with each other. Once you get married and go to your husband's house, you will remember these times you have spent with each other. That's how siblings always are. Now go to his room and talk to him." How could aunty not say that, such an aunty-ish thing to say! I was not in a mood to listen to any of it, but I guess I didn't have a choice.

Then I go to his room. He is sitting on his bed, with a pillow in his lap and staring blankly, at nothing in particular, outside the window. He looks sad too. I sit on the chair facing him. The tick-tock of the clock, on the wall behind me, seems louder and faster than ever before. As if, its master has induced the effect of his own mood into the clock as well. He doesn't speak and even doesn't look at me.

"Hey, appease that anger now. You know how much I love you," I say, and my tone sounds sad.

When I get no response from him, I continue, "I've decided to not to look at Esha again just because you mean more to me than anything else." Saying this, I sit next to him on the bed.

He still chooses not to meet my eyes or utter a single word. The silence between us stretches a little more.

I am unable to tolerate his silent treatment any more.

"Hey, say something. Don't just zip it," I say, followed by a pause for him to retort. His muteness has the volume of his anger and the sound of his disappointment caused by me. I can stand his shriek, but quietness is not for me.

I plead, "Please say something." Then I cry, looking down at my hands.

He smacks me on my head and says, "Stop that cry drama now, let's go eat something."

We eat together, but I still feel his uneasiness. I can see, in his actions, his peace of mind being stifled. The way he breaks chapatti for each bite, is way slower than I have seen him do that before.

I decide that I won't look at Esha again. I do not for three months.

CHAPTER 3. HITLER SISTER

End of March

I AM DONE WITH MY BOARD EXAMS. There is no question now of bumping into Esha. We were never friends and I don't know where she lives, what her future plans are and what not. I wish to know those things about her. But for sure I am guilty of a crime to my heart—the crime of an unexpressed love. The purpose for which I left it unexpressed, doesn't seem to get fulfilled either. I don't see things between Girish and me getting back to normal.

These last few months I have compelled myself not to think about Esha. The more I try to keep my mind free of thoughts of her, the more I crave her. The more I try to wipe her out from my memory, the more I weep in the dark. I am not sure doing this is getting me any closer to Girish either. Maybe he understands me well; that's why he can read my eyes, see the pain behind my smile that I force myself to wear. But still I continue the efforts from my side hoping everything between he and I will be back to normal soon. Perhaps, as always, I am being submissive to be loved. That's how I am. If I love someone, I love them to an extent that I never refrain to forego my identity for them. I feel lonelier day by day.

I am done with my exams. I decide to take painting classes to spend time with my hobby. Everybody in the house believes I want to spend time on painting instead of just lying down on bed. But I am not sure of the reason I am taking painting classes. Is it because I want to be away from Girish as much as possible so that he doesn't read my mind? Or do I want to keep myself busy with the other possible things I could do, except for thoughts of Esha? But Mom does not like the idea of me joining this class. She is rising a bit of a fuss about it.

From the reasons that she gives, I gather, she is worried about me going to Bandra every day just to attend the class. I, on the other hand, am super excited about going to Bandra. One reason is I will get to go there alone with nobody accompanying me, which will be fun. Before this whenever I went outside Mulund, I always went with Girish. I am eager to go by myself like a free bird. Well, perhaps I want to get submerged with the crowd and a busy schedule to get rid of the solitude that I feel nowadays. Another reason I am elated about going to Bandra is "Jai sandwich." I love their sandwiches.

The mere thought of the cilantro-mint chutney he uses for those yummy sandwiches makes me hungry. Whenever I went to Bandra with Girish and his friends, we always ate there, without fail. My painting class is only a block away from the Jai sandwich place. This means I could eat there every day.

I try hard to convince Mom. Lots of buttering her up and snuggling with her might help. I hug mom tight. "Please Mom, please, I love you. You are such a nice and sweet mommy, please let me register for the class. You know how much I love painting."

"I love you too, Beta, but no, you are not going to that class," Mom says, caressing my cheek and giving all the reasons of the world.

She is not telling the real reason yet; I could read it on her face. There is one quality of Mom I absolutely adore. She cannot lie about what she is thinking. Even if she tries to fib, a white lie—for good though, to not to hurt anyone—she cannot succeed in it. Most of the time, this is used, against her, by everybody in the extended family, but she does not mind it. She says, "At least I have peace of mind. I don't carry any heaviness in my heart and disturbances in my head. Whatever I am thinking, you guys get it out of me whether good or bad." But at times it has caused problems too.

"But, why Mom, why can't I go to that class?" I squeeze her tight, insisting, "Please, tell me." She bursts into tears without saying any more words. Every house in India has saas-bahu-ki-kahani—mother-in-law daughter-in-law stories. In our house, we have ma-beti-ki-kahani—mom-daughter stories.

Looking at those watery eyes, I am thinking, "*not again, Mom*". But I embrace her even tighter and say, "Please tell me what is going on in your mind."

"See, what did Pahal do, when we gave her liberty of going alone to Bandra College? We don't want you to do the similar kind of things. Please don't even ask me again for this class," cries Mom.

Pahal is my elder sister—less sister, more Hitler. She is five years elder to me, tall, slim, sexy—one of those TV model types. OK-OK in studies, lazy in household work, but number one in seducing boys with her killer hazel eyes and exposed cleavage.

The only common feature we both inherited from Mom's genes is hazel eyes, but each with a different gleam and different expression that it portrays.

And if there is anything else she is better at, then definitely it is torturing her little sister, that's me. Living in Mumbai, in a middle-class family, lack of space has always been a problem. Di and I shared a room; at least that is what everybody else thought. But she ruled the room as her kingdom as if she was the queen and I had to be in the room as if I didn't belong to that house at all. I had to always compromise and listen to her for two reasons, one she is Hitler and another reason is this Hitler has much support from family members. She is the honeymoon child of my parents. As a result she is extra pampered, the most lovable child at home. My mom and dad consider her their good luck. When she was born, all of a sudden Dad started doing very well in his business, which was in loss before. Thus she was the start of the good life; that's what they considered then. Hence they named her Pahal meaning start—start of the good life.

God knows, how she graduated from high school even! The way she dressed was unbelievable; she would wear tight-fitting jeans that showed her curves perfectly, with a low-cut top with her boobs ready to pop out. Mom and Dad never knew about it because she always had a cardigan on the top. That cardigan was just to show Mom and Dad; it was definitely taken off as soon as she stepped out of the house.

After her twelfth, most of the girls and boys in her friend circle decided to join MMK College of Commerce & Economics in Bandra and so did she. My parents didn't know, but I understood without a doubt; her interest was more in college boys than world economics. Oh my . . . I overheard few of her phone conversations with her classmates. The way she talked with full expressions and tone change, would trap anyone. That was on the phone; I am not sure, how animated it would have been face-to-face. Not only that, every night before going to bed, all she would talk about was "Oh . . . this boy said this to me, that one said that. Ooooo . . . that boy is so hot that I wanted to slip into his pants." I was always tired of those cheesy talks. Should I dare to say can we talk about something else but boys of your college, she would harangue me. She has always been the favorite child of the house; she took advantage of that fact and kept torturing me. According to her, it's her birth-right aka being-elder-sibling-right to say whatever she wants and I have to listen. "If that is your birth-right, excuse me, where is my self-right?" Many times I would think of it, but keep it to myself just to avoid any further torment. Being a peace lover, I, many times, kept quiet instead of blurting out my disagreement with reference to her behavior.

At first, Mom and Dad said no to her to join MMK College. They insisted she join the commerce college in Mulund itself. But then she tried flattering mom; of course she was way better than me at that. She also gave Mom and Dad lectures on being liberal. She convinced them how the world is changing and how she needs more liberty in her life to grow and what not . . . somehow my parents agreed on that. Didn't I tell you earlier, she got way around everything and everybody? She made sure to do everything else but study in college. All she wanted out of that college was to pataofy—trap a boy—to marry—from New Mumbai. Was there a doubt that she would succeed in her mission?

By mid-first year, she had a boyfriend. He went to the same class as Di. Di talked about him during our nightly ritual of her talking on guys and me listening with "interest" pretending to be curious all along. The little I understood from her conversations, he was the spoiled son of a rich dad. He gave expensive chocolates to Di every other day as Di loved the chocolates.

Liking chocolate runs in our family.

But she never shared a single piece with me. She would give the excuse that these chocolates are his love. She can't share his love with me. She stopped eating at roadside stands when she went out with him. He would take her to the expensive restaurants and classy hotels for dinner. Di always wanted to have a rich boyfriend to hang out with and then ultimately marry that boy. She thought her dream was about to come true. She thought this was "The Guy."

She started talking about him a lot at home, even with our parents. Mom always told her, "Please don't get too much involved with this guy. These rich boys; who knows what they will do to you?" Mom was always scared, thanks to olden days Hindi cinema.

Not that every rich child is spoiled, but moms worry. Mom is Mom. Worrying for her child is the gift every mom gets with a child.

Di and this guy started staying out late. They would go to pubs and have fun. She would come home late at around 10:00 PM. Mom and Dad would get heated up dealing with her late arrivals. Her excuse was, "We are only friends and study partners. We were studying late at his house." Our parents believed in her lies. I knew the truth. But I never let her secrets out to anyone because I loved her. And I always believed these gestures might help foster a good sibling relationship between us. I wonder how she never understands that, even now.

Regarding me joining the painting class—I cannot convince Mom. I wait the entire day for dad to come home. Even before he comes home, I picture him entering the house, as usual, touching his pot belly and calling out from the entry door, "I am starving. What's for dinner today?"

Growing up, I have seen Dad transforming from being a handsome, health nut young man to an uncle with a little bit of a belly. But he still leaves his impression on people around him of having a tall body frame and wide shoulders. When I tease him about his belly, he says "Age is catching up with me." But he knows by all means that he needs to walk more. Sitting in his shop the whole day combined with a diet of buttery food is causing a disaster. Dad always thinks pragmatic, unlike Mom who is emotional. Sometimes I wish Dad's practical thinking trait should have been dominant in me instead of Mom's sensitive, submissive, and emotional nature.

In spite of what happened with Di, he never restricts me from taking part in the activities of my interests, especially painting. He has always wished that Di and I would both study and become independent one day. Di couldn't do that. I will not let him down. I want to make him proud. But many times, in fulfilling aspirations of others, in making people around me happy, I bury my own wishes to not let it surface in the way of desires of my loved one's. Unknowingly I have been feeding my mind with the pernicious thought; *I have to be submissive to be loved*. Now I understand that it is not right. But I continue the same submissive behavior because I never practiced any other way. This is who I am. This is how I recognize myself.

Dad talks Mom into letting me go to the painting class.

*****

I can't wait to go to class. Next day, the first thing I do, I call Passion Painting Studio to register for the class. A sweet voice answers the phone. After she has enrolled me, she asks me to visit the studio website to learn what materials I have to buy for oil painting. In excitement, I forget that we don't have a computer and internet at home to visit a website. Duh! I call them again to get the list of things.

"Bring with you an 18 X 20-inch hardboard. A citrus thinner and a small bottle of linseed oil," she said. I wonder why linseed oil.

"Also buy a palette, a palette knife, and brush set," she continues.

"Brush set?" I ask.

"Yeah, you don't know . . . Oh, a bristle flat brush set. Make sure it has brushes 1 1/4 inches wide, 1 inch wide, 3/4 inches wide, and two brushes, 1/2 inch wide. Sable flat brushes 1/2 inch wide, 1/4 inch wide, and two sizes of small rounds."

"What about colors?" I inquire.

"Yes, pick any color you like. Most students pick a large tube of Titanium White and smaller tubes of Cadmium yellow pale, Cadmium Orange, Cadmium Red, Quinacridone Rose, Dioxazine Violet, French Ultramarine Blue, and Cadmium Green," she says.

I did not realize until now spelling colors would be this difficult. I scribble the approximate close spelling on a chit.

*****

Sunday

Before the class starts, Dad is home. Sunday is the day off for him. His shop is closed. After the scrumptious lunch of mutton curry served with hot chapatti and side course of onion mixed with salt and lemon, we go to buy the materials for my painting class. Mom doesn't want to come with us. She wants to finish her everyday household chores. Satisfied and content with the ravishing taste of mutton curry, I feel the same tenderness in my tone as that of the meat of today's curry when I plead with Mom to come with us. "Mom, you and I will finish it faster together after returning home. Come with us, please," I insist.

CHAPTER 4. THE UNEXPECTED ALWAYS HAPPENS

Monday morning

I AM ALL READY TO LEAVE for the first day of my class. Mom insists on a heavy breakfast for me that way I can survive five to six hours without eating anything. By the time I come back home it will be closer to 3:00 PM.

Dad comments, "Eat and then carry a little extra snack with you. You never know when Mumbai restaurants, food-selling street vendors, and food stalls on local stations would run out of foodstuff." Dad and I give a hearty chuckle; got to love his sense of humor.

Mom mutters, "Yeah, Pahal's dad, tease me as much as you want. And Soni, you too, huh?"

Without hurting her feelings any more, I eat aloo paratha—stuffed potato chapatti—with plain yogurt and leave home to catch the 10:00 AM fast local for Dadar. I am excited to travel all by myself and nervous as well to board the train. If you have never traveled in a local train before in Mumbai, picture a jam-packed train cabin where people are hanging on the doors because there is no more place to enter in. I have realized it is more an art to board these trains than anything ordinary. An art the daily commuters are proficient at and non-frequent travelers like me are uninformed about. The train only stops at a station for mere seconds. If you wait for your turn to board, you will never be able to ride.

I throw myself at the gate of a ladies compartment; I get squeezed into the train by the crowd of irritated office goers behind me. The whole compartment smells of fish and human sweat. I try to ignore the smell and poke my head up above the crowd so I do not suffocate. Soon I realize that everybody else is doing the same; it is not helping. My heart is thumping for the whole thirty minutes till I reach Dadar station. Half of my travel is done—a proud moment; I pat myself on the back. This is my first time traveling in a local all by myself. Now, I board another local for Bandra. This one is not as crowded since I am going away from the downtown. In this train, I see a group of women chatting animatedly among themselves and a group of girls playing antakshari—an interactive singing game.

A hawker—a boy barely twelve years old selling trinkets stops by and puts his puppy eyes on me, "*Madam, ye ear rings achha lagenga aapape*—these earrings would look nice on you."

When I smile without saying a word, he tries harder, "Please, madam . . . le lo na—buy it please."

The way he says it, I feel sorry for what he has to do. I feel sorry that he has lost his childhood in the local train selling those trinkets, instead of going to school or playing with kids of his age. At that moment, I thank God for the good life I have. I realize that our busy competitive lives have taken away the content and gratitude for what we have. Instead we always are hungry for more. While thinking all this, I rummage through my bag and take out a ten rupee note to buy the earrings from him. But when I look up to hand the money to him, he has already disappeared in the crowd. Everybody around me seems to be in a rush. In the next few minutes, I see a woman hawker carrying a basket full of flowers. I notice one thing; the hawkers do not stay for long in one compartment. They hop on to the next compartment or catch another train to sell their goods.

By the time I reach Bandra, I am weary. I am not tired as much from holding that heavy bag with the easel or 18 by 20 inch hardboard as of the hard massage that I got in the train. Ugh! Not fun.

On my way from Bandra station to the painting studio, I can barely contain my excitement to learn oil painting, meet my instructor, and dive into the world of colors. I imagine what the studio will be like. I have seen shabby-looking studios in the past. The one near my house where I learned to paint in my early childhood was a small, untidy, and crowded studio with many paintings drying on one side of the room, tables and chairs on the other side, small items of clothing—used for wiping the remnants of the color from painting brushes—hanging from the armrests of the chairs or kept on a table top. I picture something similar. I don't realize when I reach the studio in Bandra, but instead I think I have entered the wrong place. I am about to take a U-turn when my eyes fall on a few easels set up opposite to a parade of windows on my right-hand side. Then soon I apprehend the receptionist sitting on the left side of the entry door. She is on the phone.

I can't envision this place being a painting studio, where hundreds of kids come to learn to paint from 7:00 in the morning to 9:00 in the night. I see no signs of portraits that are left for drying; no paint-covered clothes dangling around. It is a big L-shaped room, extremely neat and clean. The short line of the L is where the receptionist is sitting. The longer line of the L has a parade of windows on one side of the room. Six easels—each with a drawer attached to it—are sitting quiet, set up opposite to the windows, two hands' distance apart from one another. There is one more easel. This seventh easel is a little crowded with a half-done piece of work and wet paint brushes are resting on the small tray attached to it. On careful observation, I notice, those quietly sitting six easels have signs of paint on the attached trays. The wall opposite to the windows is an astonishing work of art. This long wall has a painting of a short and fat tree, with numerous faces hanging from the tree branches. Each face has a unique expression as if each expression represents a human emotion.

By now my hands hurt from holding the heavy hardboard. Looking at such a clean and nicely done room, a number of thoughts run through my head leaving me startled. *Do I have to take my hardboard back home every single day? I don't want to carry the hardboard every day in that packed train.*

After a little pause, more contemplation makes me go nuts. *I can't take the wet painting home either. Oil paint doesn't dry soon. What am I thinking?*

My crazy thoughts are interrupted by the noise of chit chatting. Four boys enter the room. I figure these are my painting classmates. While we exchange names, our instructor comes to the receptionist's desk from behind me, from the part of the room where I was eyeing a minute ago. I get scared; a spooky question explodes in my mind, *How come I didn't see him when I was looking at that side of the room! What's going on?* I let go of that thought to concentrate on what he says.

"Hi, I am Kabir," the instructor starts. "There is one more student who is supposed to join us. I guess she must be late. Let's start the class."

I am amused to see the tree that is painted on the wall. Looking at the painting, "Wow!" is all that I can say, when Kabir sir opens the door. The trunk of that tree mural is a door to another room where the students' art pieces are kept for drying. Even the door knob is part of the tree trunk. You cannot realize it unless you see someone go through. It reminds me of Harry Potter going to platform 9¾ to catch the Hogwarts Express. That entire wall is decorated by Kabir sir. It is a superb example of his finest work.

Without him telling us, no one could figure out that there is a room inside. We enter that room. Inside it is nothing like the outside. It is dark in here with only a dim light on. As we enter the room, we see three walls of the room are lined with built-in wooden shelves, at two different height levels. The entire painting inventory—paints, oil paint remover, dilute solutions and many other required materials—is kept in one closet, standing tall in the middle of the room. Many half-done paintings are drying there. Few fully done portraits are waiting to get hung on the walls of somebody's drawing room. The fourth wall of the room, on the left side of the door as we enter, has a series of hooks, again at two different height levels to hang the pieces of cloths used for wiping off paint from the painting brush. On the right side of the door, a long gray marble counter top holds a tan-colored sink and two water taps.

I ask, "Why are we given a list to buy the oil painting materials and easel when we use everything from here?" Kabir sir just looks at me. His eyes rest on me, and he smiles. I almost have my tongue sticking out in embarrassment for asking that silly question. *How would we work on our assignments at home?* I realize.

After showing us the dark room, he takes us out and asks us to set up our stuff on any empty easel. Each one of us grabs one. One last in line and next to me is still empty. The sixth student hasn't arrived yet. Kabir sir stands next to the seventh easel which still holds the half-done painting. He speaks with each of us, asking questions to understand our overall painting skills. Everybody seems to have done painting before, but none of us have done oil painting yet.

While the class is in session, the sixth student comes, half an hour late. This is the first day; we haven't really started anything significant yet. Kabir sir goes to the newly arrived student while I set up my things.

"Sonia, would you mind showing Esha where to grab materials from the dark room." requests Kabir sir.

Esha! Oh crap! I think.

"Please GOD, not the same Esha, pleaaaaaaaaaaaaase ..." I mutter under my breath.

"Sonia, are you OK with that?" asks Kabir sir.

"Yes, sir," I reply, walking toward the wall to go the room. I enter the dark room followed by her. I turn around to gaze at her; the glance takes my breath away. Hiding my nervousness, I show her around. I show her where to grab the jar from and where the water tap is. We both come out of the dark room in the order we went in.

Class continues for the next forty-five minutes, but I can't concentrate. Most of the class he talks about the oil painting supplies, explaining the usage of each material we bought. My mind by now is tempted to turn back and catch a glimpse of Esha. I somehow resist the temptation, but still cannot concentrate. Good that he will talk about it again as and when we need to use the materials in the class.

The last fifteen minutes, everybody cleans their painting brushes, palette, puts away the hardboard, piece of cloth, and empties the jar of water and sets these back where we picked them up. No wonder this place is kept super clean. Everybody takes and fulfills a bit of the responsibility to keep it neat.

*****

I finish my part of clean up hastily. Pick up my bag and start off to the station as fast as I can. Seeing her in the same class was unexpected. I didn't think, even once, that she could come to this class. *Life is full of surprises. The unexpected always happens*, I whisper in my mind. I am not sure why, but I believe talking to Esha will make me emotionally vulnerable and I do not want to be in that situation.

I press the elevator button and it takes time to come. Thus I walk down the stairs to avoid speaking to her. Three floors down, I am tired. *Four more to go . . . this is exhausting*, I think while I jump down from one step to another. The surroundings of the stairs look horrible. On the fourth floor, in a corner— where the stairs from the fifth to the fourth floor and the stairs from the fourth to the third floor meet— something is written in bold and a big font in bright red color. "*Krupaya paan khakar yahan na thuke.* Please do not spit paan here." Paan is an ethnic Indian chew. It is rolled up in a small green betel leaf with a variety of sweet or savory fillings in the middle which can include but is not limited to rose syrup, saffron, cardamom, and coconut. Paan is usually eaten after a meal to aid digestion and freshen the mouth. Chewing paan is kind of addiction that brings many drawbacks with it.

One of which has caused the sign "*Krupaya paan khakar yahan na thuke*" to be halfway covered with red stains. It is sad how people spit paan right at the spot where the sign to not spit is painted. I have seen it everywhere in public places. But a sea of people around made me ignore those stains. Walking alone and the lack of sunshine on the stairs make those stains noticeable. The sight grosses me out, and I speed up. I am glad I took the elevator in the morning and I decide to do the same from now on. I breathe a sigh of relief as I reach the ground floor. I stroll steadily towards the station to avoid being seen by Esha.

After covering half the distance, I feel somebody is following me. At first, I consider my mind is making something up. But, I sense it once more. This time I turn to look who it is. It's her. She walks fast as well. I stride even faster than her. We both not only happen to catch the same train but also sit next to each other. Well, I sat first, and then she parked herself in an empty space next to me. I cannot do much about it.

"Hi, I am Esha," she says extending her hand for me to shake.

I fumble. *I am going to that painting class so that my painting-occupied mind will prevent me from thinking about you. But here you come extending your hand. Oh God . . . what is happening?* I ponder, still silent.

"Oh! Hi, I am Sonia," I reply with a wry smile. When her fingers touch mine, a cold wave runs through my body, making me fumble even more. "You—-you can call me Soni. All my close family and friends do."

Stupid! What are you saying . . . control yourself . . . forget about close; she is not even your friend. You don't want to talk to her. Remember what Girish said. Just k-e-e-p quiet n-o-w, my conscious mind, which doesn't want to talk to her, scolds me. After that we don't exchange a single word till we reach Dadar.

As soon as we get off the train, I move faster to go to another platform to catch my train to Mulund. I can hear my heart beat, loud and rapid. *Is it because of her? Or because I am walking fast?* I wonder.

Anyways . . . she tries to keep up with my strolling speed.

"Have you ever tried Dadar station's lassi?" she inquires, catching her breath.

Thinking about a sip of cold yogurt smoothie on a hot summer afternoon makes me fall for her offer. But somehow I resist myself.

"I am in a hurry. I have no time for lassi," I reply bluntly.

Even though I never meant to be rude to her, those blunt words came out of me as I was trying to avoid her while still having feelings for her.

I rush to another platform leaving her behind and promising myself not to think about her again. My heart and mind keep contradicting each other for her. I am glad that my mind took over my heart this time. Running away from her seemed easier.

Finally home, I remove the table top easel from my bag and feel delighted that from tomorrow I don't have to carry it. I take a quick shower, eat food. An evening is equally exciting helping mom in the kitchen in making dinner followed by painting class talk with Dad. Dad listens to every bit with interest. After dinner, Dad watches his news channel, Mom cleans up in the kitchen, and I go to Girish's house to find out he is not home. He is studying at a friend's house for his upcoming exams. I wanted to share everything relating to my today's class with him. I want him to visit my painting class to see Kabir sir's amazing mural and the arrangement of the L-shaped studio. But a thought follows me from his house to my bed, *if he visits the studio that means he might see Esha there too. No, I don't want that.* I lay down on the bed, saying "Good, he is not home."

I am obsessed with the painted wall of the studio. I can't stop thinking about it. I wonder, how many days did he take to finish that mural? Did he finish it in one go without taking breaks for hours together? His arms, back and who knows, his every body part must have hurt when he finished it.

Tired from the whole day of rushing around, I close my eyes to relax. With shut eyes, I see her face. I quickly open my eyes and stare at the ceiling fan, which is moving faster than ever before. Having her in the same class as me will not help in my mission of keeping her off my thoughts. But then I may not get the lifetime chance again to learn painting from a great artist like Kabir sir. I contradict my one thought with another multiple times before reaching any resolution.

The question wiggles my mind. *Should I deregister myself from the painting class?* Still trying to answer my question, I am not sure when I shut my eyes and fall sleep.

CHAPTER 5. CHIT CHAT QUEEN

The next morning

I WAKE UP WITH THE SPIRIT to start a new day. I am in a good mood. I am comfortable until I reach the class. I enter the studio and there she is, waving a big hi at me, wearing a wide cheery smile on her face.

Oh boy, why does this girl have to be drop-dead gorgeous? I am about to say. Instead, I reply with a plain hi. She is wearing light blue jeans and a bright red top with shining silver studs in her ears. Hair tied up high in a ponytail. The red color contrasts with her so-very-perfect skin tone. The wide V-neck of the top shows off her prominent clavicle bones. No wonder the clavicle bone is called the beauty bone of girls. I never liked this bright red color as much before. This girl wreaks havoc in my mind. My heart melts at a glimpse of her. Merely taking a look at her, from the corner of my eyes, makes me forget what I was thinking. The more I want to keep my mind off her, the stronger the grip she is setting on my heart. I clench my fist tight with the thought I will not think about her any more.

The other students have not arrived yet. I go to the dark room to get my hardboard and other stuff I need. She follows me. "I can help you, Soni, if you don't mind. I am done setting my things already."

"No thanks, I can take care of it myself," I say, shunning her.

"Are you OK? Yesterday also, you were talking in the same weird way when I asked you about lassi."

When she says that, I realize I have been unintentionally rude to her.

"Sorry, I don't mean to. I am not in a good mood these days," I apologize politely this time.

"Then we must go for ice cream after the class to cheer you up." hearing her say that I curse myself for conversing with her all over again. I wonder, *is she always that chatty with everybody, or is it just me because I am the only girl, other than her, of course, in the class?* The boys of our class enter the dark room to fetch their things and I let Esha hold a few supplies for me without talking to her any further. After setting up the painting materials on my easel, I thank her for the help. She doesn't say you are welcome, but her soothing smile makes my day.

On the earlier day, after applying three coats of primer followed by sanding, we had divided the hardboard into four zones, to use each zone to practice different lessons. The first lesson is on basic forms.

"Different brush strokes are used for each form. Remember, triangular strokes help with cones, crescent strokes work for sphere and torus. Use curved strokes for sphere, torus and then circular blends. Parallel strokes help make cylinders and the faces of a cube," Kabir sir explains. "As we move along in this exercise, you will learn about all the painting materials. By the end of this exercise, you will learn how to use the paints and brushes in the different ways."

Kabir sir spends individual time with each student to re-teach the strokes. He also watches each one of us doing those strokes and gives us feedback. I enjoy the class and lose track of time. It feels like the class ends too soon. I put away all my things in the dark room in proper places. The last thing remaining is to empty the jar of water.

"So . . . , are you ready for ice cream?" Esha's voice comes from behind. I want to say no, but instead I convince myself to go. *Just go with her as her friend . . . no more no less!* I think in my head, nodding to her. She raises the jar in excitement and cheers, "Yes!"

Self-interrogations, one after another, drive me crazy. Up until yesterday I was determined not to talk to her and now I am ready to go for ice cream date with her—*Ya, ya, not exactly a date*, I tell myself. I put a pause on all those ongoing questions and jump in to enjoy my little time with her. We go out of the building and cross the road making our way through traffic to Amul ice cream parlor.

Esha starts the conversation. She keeps talking non-stop, while we are crossing the road, while we are waiting for ice cream and of course while eating it too. She seems to have this remarkable energy to keep going on forever. When we reach the ice cream parlor, she asks, "I will have black current. What will you have? Which is your favorite ice cream flavor?"

Even before I could say anything, she reads out loud all the flavors from the big menu at the door. I let her finish and say, "Chocolate!"

"Uncle, two scoops black current and chocolate ice cream in cones, please," she says paying the money to the elderly person sitting on the other side of the counter. When I take out the wallet from my bag; she holds my hand dragging me to the other end of the counter to get ice cream and declares, "This time it's on me, but next time on you."

I am stunned, looking at her big almond-shaped sparkling eyes and her astounding exuberance. After listening to her for a while, I am awed.

"Soni, Soni," she snaps fingers in front of my lost eyes, which have gone astray watching her, as she mesmerizes me. That snap brings me back to her conversation. "It seems something is going on in your mind. Everything all right?"

"Oh, yes . . . yes," I fumble, eating the last bite of cone. I can't remember where all of my ice cream went.

"I think we should get going now; my mom will be worried if I don't reach home in time," I say to avoid any further investigation on her 'Everything all right?' question.

"If you say so," Esha says.

"I am silly, I kept talking about myself. Never asked anything about you," she continues while getting up from the chair. On our way to the station, I tell her about my family. She is excited to know that I have an elder sister. She shares that she is an only child, her dad a mechanical engineer and mom an elementary school teacher. Most of the time she is at home alone because both her parents go to work.

I am sad for her. I think she misses not having siblings. Even though, Di is annoying and bossy, at that moment I feel blessed to have her. I don't mention anything with reference to Girish and his parents to her; I don't know why.

When we reach the station and are waiting for the train, she says, "I live in Mulund East, Neelam Nagar–Phase One. What about . . ."

"Hey, how about we drink lassi at Dadar station tomorrow?" I interrupt her. I don't want to exchange my whereabouts with her. I am too scared that she might show up at my home one day and what if Girish sees her with me.

"That sounds awesome!" she says, giving me a high-five. Today more people are crowding to go to Dadar station from Bandra than yesterday. Maybe because of the different time, today we are one hour late, all fault of our ice cream party. I hope to escape from her question on where I live. Luckily, we don't get seats to sit side by side like the earlier day.

*****

After reaching home, I quickly run to the kitchen and stand behind Mom while she is busy arranging the cleaned dishes. I share with her about my class, new friend, and ice cream. She is glad that finally I have made friends on my own. And I am thankful that she doesn't ask my friend's name because to my surprise, when I turn around to go back to my room, Girish is standing right behind me. The main door of our house was left open because Mom knew he will be home soon from his first subject pre-final exam of second year. After every exam, he always comes home first and tells us about how it was. He has been sharing his exam details with us for years now. This time the only difference than previous times is, he gives a summary instead of details and the whole time he looks at Mom and speaks. Then he leaves quickly without saying a word. I go back to my room, sitting quietly, reflecting; *is he still enraged at me? Did I not say I won't look at Esha because I love him more than anything else in the world?*

Well, I am not keeping the promise completely, but he doesn't have a clue about it yet. Why the heck is he behaving odd with me again? I muse. The entire evening I am annoyed at him for his behavior, but I couldn't share that with anyone around here. It seems as if he built the wall around him. The wall to avoid talking to me. The wall to keep him away from me. I don't come out of my room for the rest of the evening.

Why should I worry about him this much when he doesn't even care for me anymore? What did I do wrong? I just said she is mine. I did nothing wrong. The turmoil gives me a headache and provokes a rebellious teenager that is somewhere inside me too like every other teenager. If he doesn't care about me, about his sister anymore, why should I? A bout of thoughts continue in my mind. *Esha is becoming a good friend and I could easily tell her about . . .*

Suddenly, the calm and composed side of me interrupts the rebellious, stubborn side. *Easy . . . easy. It's just a phase which will pass away soon. We are simply friends, no more. You do not want to blow it away, do you?*

I want to stop the cascade of thoughts that were blowing my mind. I get up from my bed and go to the kitchen for a glass of water, hit the bathroom and get back in my cozy, comfy bed.

Chapter 6. Just a friend

In painting class

WE CONTINUE LEARNING NEW STROKES. We learn how to use colors, the medium to mix with colors to get different effects in painting. It goes along well. Kabir sir mentions that this weekend's homework will be based on basic forms. After the class, Esha and I stride out together to go to the station. While walking on the crowded road, her hand touches mine twice. The first time it touches, I move my hand closer to myself with lightning speed, saying "I'm sorry."

She mocks my gesture, "Are you always like this, extra cautious and conservative? Or do you only behave weird seeing me?"

My jaw drops and my mouth remains open. She laughs out louder and spanks me on my hand, saying, "That was a joke, you silly!"

This time I join in her giggle too. Mine is not as hearty as hers. I don't know what is happening to me—otherwise a carefree and brave girl is shy when near her. Soon we reach the lassi stall at Dadar station. Today, time runs so fast in her company. This time I pay for the lassi. After taking a first sip of it, I tell her where I live.

"Noooo way you live in Phase-2," she screams, flabbergasted. "You live only few blocks away from my house."

As soon as we finish drinking the lassi, she holds my hand and runs to catch the next local for Mulund, which we don't want to miss. She commands that from tomorrow we will come to class together and accompany each other going back home. I nod, giving in. Cocktail feelings lurch my stomach. On one hand, I am scared—while walking home, what if Girish sees us together—and on the other hand I feel blissful having her by my side. I return home overjoyed for the time that I have spent with her. I look forward to go to class the next day.

In the morning, I reach the station ten minutes earlier than usual. I don't want to miss any chance to hang out with her. Killing those ten minutes gets difficult. I stare at all the girls coming down the stairs, in the hope to see her soon. I end up waiting twenty minutes. Wow, I am surprised; I never knew I could wait for anyone with patience. I think I could wait for that long because I was controlled by hope;

aren't we all? Hope to see loved ones if they live miles away, hope to find the only one who is for you, hope to be surrounded by people who you like the most and many more. Esha does not show up. At last, I leave alone for the class.

Couldn't she wait for me a little longer? Feels like I am crazy to wait for her for that long. I am mad at her, I guess; I was looking forward to spending more time with her. I reach class five minutes late. But she is not there either.

Now, I curse myself under my breath, "Couldn't I wait a little longer?"

But she doesn't show up for the class that day. I worry, secretly hoping that she is not sick. Then, I wish, we should have exchanged our phone numbers. I have a landline at home and she carries a cell phone. I can't stop my mind, which is running everywhere to think about what must have happened to her. *What if she doesn't show up for the class tomorrow too*?

On my way home, I think only about her.

*****

Friday

I am somewhat sad. For the next two days we will not have any class, and I won't be able to see Esha. When I cover half the distance to the station, I wonder, *What if she doesn't come for class today?* I slow down.

I relish being around her. But I am also afraid to express my feelings for her. Instead I have been trying to close the door of potential friendship. I decide to keep my fears at bay for once. I also resolve in my mind that, going forward, I won't stop myself from communicating my feelings to her, and it's worth a try. If I don't try it, then nothing will ever work my way. She has been friendly with me from the first day of class. I am the one who has closed herself in a shell in Girish's name. By being friendly, is she trying to give me a cue that she likes me too, I reckon. (After a small pause) I laugh at myself. *You are thinking little too much, girlie.*

In a jiffy, a soft hand, that seems recently manicured, wearing turquoise-colored nail paint, touches my shoulder, leaving me scared only for less than a second till I turn around to see who it is.

"Where were you yesterday?" I demand, holding her soft hand.

"Oh no . . . sorry! I forgot to tell you," she says, biting her tongue. Then continues, "I went for my cousin's engagement."

"You know how long I was waiting for you at the station," I say, gently moving my thumb over her fingers and nails. Her fingers feel soft and touchable. Instead of getting mad at her, for not informing me about her not coming to class, I am more willing to reconcile with her.

"Hey, seems you like my nail paint?" she says now, holding my hand and walking toward the station.

"Yes, it's beautiful. What did you wear for your cousin's engagement ceremony?" I ask.

"I wore a turquoise color saree with sequins and silver bead-embroidered border. I also wore silver and turquoise bangles and long leaf-shaped silver stone earrings that looked perfect with my saree," she explains. She keeps chirping the whole time. She talks about the fun time she had yesterday. I enjoy seeing her happy, in a perfect Esha-ish way.

When we board the train, we don't get to sit next to each other. Where I am sitting, I can see her broad shoulders, thin neck, and head. I keep staring in her direction. *How stunning she must have looked in her turquoise saree*, I think in my head. I picture her wearing a wide smile, as she always does, to greet her friends and family. Suddenly, I have this strong desire to be by her side, to take part in family event together.

"Soni, let's go," says Esha. I didn't realize when we reached our destination.

It is getting difficult to concentrate in class. We finish the small piece of work that we started on Tuesday.

"As homework, this weekend, practice basic forms of painting with different shapes than what we have painted in the class," declares Kabir sir.

"Have you bought the hardboard for homework?" Esha asks while we walk out of the class side-by-side, our steps moving in unison forming a pattern of its own.

"No. I haven't," I reply.

"Cool, then we both can go together to buy it," she calls out.

"Yes, sure and then we can do homework together, maybe at your place," I add.

"Sounds like a plan!" she says, clasping me in excitement.

As planned, in the evening, we go to buy hardboards. We buy a few extras for more homework to come.

Our hands loaded with hardboards, we try to stop an auto rickshaw—three-wheeler public transportation.

Hard luck! Couldn't get one to stop for around twenty minutes. Finally, we both shout coherently from the place where we are standing and waiting for an auto rickshaw, "Neelam Nagar, Neelam Nagar . . . ."

Our shouting gets mixed with the voices of other people's outcry. "'Mulund West', 'Apana Bazar', 'Thane'..."

This is how the process goes for getting a rickshaw in Mumbai. When you are shouting, if you are lucky, an auto rickshaw driver will look at you. If he looks at you, then the chances of him accepting your request over others is far more. But I guess, it is not our fortunate day today. At last we walk in the opposite direction of where we have to go. All this hassle is just to stop one of the auto rickshaws. Finally, one rickshaw driver, an elderly person, looks at us and nods his head toward the back seat. That means he has agreed to go to Neelam Nagar. We are used to this routine. But today it feels like an exhausting experience, especially when we are carrying heavy loads of hardboards. It gives us a sense of a great accomplishment when we push ourselves into the back seat after almost forty minutes of struggle. Phew!

The auto rickshaw drops me at my place and then goes on to drop Esha at her place. I give one of my hardboards to her to take. After putting the remaining hardboards in their proper place at home, I inform Mom that I am going to Esha's place to do homework together.

"Eat something first and then go," Mom insists.

"No, I am not hungry, Mom." I scribble Esha's phone number for her on a piece of paper.

"Here, Esha's number if you need to call me," I say, handing her the slip of paper. I pick up all my painting material hastily along with the table top easel and leave. Mom insists more, "Eat a little before you go." I decline it and step out of the house at lightning speed.

I ring the doorbell and hear bhau . . . bhau—dog barking doorbell sound—coming from inside, which makes me smile. A beautiful lady, maybe the same age as my mom, opens the door. But she looks well-groomed compared to my mom. She is wearing a magenta pure georgette saree. It has green and purple feathers sparsely printed on it. The pattern on the saree itself is great enough to magnetize the eyes. She looks stylish in that saree. She has a mangalsutra—a kind of necklace that is a symbol of the marriage union in India—at her throat, and a mango-shaped magenta color bindi—a decoration—on her forehead. Her hair is partitioned in the middle, loosely braided down the back, and at the start of her hair partition line she wears sindoor—a vermilion line showing she is married. Now, I know, from where Esha has been gifted with those attractive looks and style.

"Hello aunty," I say before I enter.

"Sonia?"

"Yes aunty," I reply.

"Hello Beta-kiddo, have a seat," aunty says, leading me to a sofa.

"Do you want anything to drink? Water, tea or coffee?" she asks.

"No aunty. I am good."

Her house is well decorated. Living room walls painted light yellow. A tan color leather sofa with steel legs blends well with the room décor. Sunset light peering from the balcony door adds a shade of orange in the room. An oval-shaped tinted glass top coffee table adds a perfect contemporary appearance to the room. On the other side of the entry door, one wall is painted a darker shade of yellow. A triangular top dining table with six chairs is positioned opposite to this wall. The glass color and frame of the dining table are similar to the coffee table. This wall is given a personalized touch with family pictures hanging in thick bordered frames of black color and different sizes.

When Esha enters the living room, I compliment her, "Your house is beautiful and impressive."

"Courtesy of my dear mom!" she replies, pointing at her; Esha's mom smiles.

I follow Esha to her room. "Let's set up your easel first and apply primer," she commands, pointing to the study table. We apply the primer. After a few minutes, she steps out to ask her mom to make snack for us.

Her room looks spacious; in fact her whole house looks more spacious than ours. Her room walls are purple. White furniture, purple bed sheet, two pillows neatly laid out and separated by three stuffed animals complement the ambiance of the room. Many of her childhood pictures hang smilingly on the wall, unlike my house where my parents have never spent money on decorating the house. Her room has one big window that is open right now. A white easel sits in a corner near the window. I can't avoid noticing the dark purple, shimmering curtains.

"Will you girls eat Poha (flattened rice)?" her mom asks.

"Yes, we will" she says, coming in and slightly pushing the door to close. A strand of hair, from a loosely tied pony tail, falling on her face makes her look even more striking. An evening breeze blows in through her room window, making her hair strand wave gently. "Your room is nice. I love your house. It is as beautiful as you," I say, looking into her eyes.

"That means you will come often to my house then," she says, smiling back. She starts chirping again, "Can we continue our homework now?" She touches her hardboard to check whether the primer is dry. It is not yet completely dry. Then she comes to check my hardboard and stands next to me. She smells good. To touch the hardboard, her hand goes past my neck so closely that I almost feel it on me. It sends butterflies through my stomach like crazy. I glance at her; her pink lips look tender, soft and irresistible. My heart races.

Before I realize what I am doing, I turn around, hold her, and press my lips against hers. For a fraction of a second, she closes her eyes. The next moment, she pushes me away from her and paces to her hardboard. She is quiet. Somehow, I gather my courage and slowly walk to her.

"I don't know how that happened," I say, wiping my sweaty palms on my T-shirt.

She says nothing except, "Shssh! Please go," with widely opened eyes that ooze anger and disappointment.

I leave her room and her house without talking. While stepping out of the door, I heard aunty asking her, "Why is she leaving suddenly? Poha is almost done; she should have it and then go."

"It was getting late for her to go home," Esha replies back, softly, to her mom.

On my way home, I sit on the bench next to a parking lot in our apartment complex with tears in my eyes. I cry. I don't know what else to do. I am not ashamed of what I did, but I fear losing her. I hope she doesn't stop talking to me.

After some time I settle down, drag myself to the lift, step in, close the door, and press four to go home. I walk straight to my room. I don't want to eat. I lie to Mom that I ate at Esha's house. After that, I lay on the bed with my face buried in a pillow and head buried in what happened today at her house.

I know I shouldn't have kissed her like that, suddenly. But the truth be told, it was out of my control too. Only when she pushed me did I realize what had happened, let alone how it happened.

Then again I visualize how it was and feel those butterflies yet again running through my stomach. I smile coyly.

No matter what her reaction was later, she did enjoy the kiss, she reciprocated. Otherwise she wouldn't have closed her eyes, I muse. "I need to talk to her right now," I say loudly to myself and get out of the bed to make a call. The clock on my bed side ticks 10:00 PM. Ignoring the clock, I call her, expecting to be disappointed. She doesn't pick up in spite of my three calls.

CHAPTER 7. CUPID'S ARROW MAKES ITS MARK

Next Morning

I CALL HER TWICE to no avail. I curse myself all over again for what happened yesterday. I don't want to come out of my room. I don't want to talk to anyone anymore. I don't want to do anything.

In another half an hour, our landline rings. I wait for Mom to pick up.

"It's yours, Soni," Mom reports.

I jump out of my bed. In response to my hello, I hear a bleak voice I am not used to hearing.

"I am at home. You can come and take your painting material." Esha sounds confused and mad at me.

"OK," I say. After a long pause I add, "Does that mean we are not doing homework together again?"

"I don't know," she responds. "Got to go!" she says and hangs up before I can utter another word.

After breakfast, I go to her house. This time she opens the door and leads me to her room and points to my stuff. I feel I am experiencing an alter ego of Esha; her cheerful exuberance is not near her today. She is quiet, and I get the impression she is thinking a lot about something.

"I seriously don't know what happened yesterday. I promise it won't happen again," I break down while ruefully packing my stuff.

She remains silent.

"Please say something," I plead.

She says nothing. When I turn around to leave, she holds my bag. I freeze.

"Where are you going? Don't you have to finish your homework," she says in a soft voice.

I turn around in disbelief, saying, "That means you are not mad at me anymore, are you?"

"I was never mad at you," she replies with same monotonous tone that she has been maintaining since morning.

"Then why didn't you reply to my calls?" I question.

Once again silence fills the room, awakening a weird fright within me. The silence is dreadful.

"Esha, why?" I say, going closer to her.

She breaks the hush uttering, "I like you." My heart beats faster. In a jiffy, I imagine my whole life with her.

"But . . ." she continues, only to stop. Then she walks toward the wall of her room where her pictures are hanging. She stares at those pictures.

"But . . . what?" I ask, following her to the wall.

When she doesn't retort back for a while, I ask, "Do you have a boyfriend?"

She replies instantly, "No, I don't." She turns around to look at me and fumbles, "I like you, but . . . I mean . . . I am . . . I am confused."

She hesitates, but continues after a small pause, "Can we not be only friends?"

Since yesterday the scare of losing her has been slowly killing me. "OK, friends!" I jump on the opportunity. At least she will be close. At least I will get to see her. I smile and set my stuff on her table. I settle myself, thinking—*it is not necessary that she has to love me if I love her. Maybe she has a different perspective of things. She is not sure about it from her side, but she didn't say no.* That still keeps a ray of hope alive in me.

After finishing a part of the homework, we eat spicy eggplant curry with freshly cooked steamed rice for lunch at her house. The texture of the cooked eggplant is perfect, the spices in the right amounts. I have never eaten this delicious eggplant-peanut curry before.

"Wow aunty, yummy eggplant. I need to get the recipe from you for my mom," I compliment her. The joy of having yummy food is revealed clearly on my face. Sitting at the dining table, we decide that today and tomorrow afternoon, we will continue with our homework and try to finish it.

After food, Esha and I proceed to her room to continue painting.

*****

Second week of the class
This week we concentrate on color shades. Kabir sir gives us a picture of a group of vegetables and asks us to draw and color them as oil painting on the hardboard. "In this exercise, the colors are seen only as lights and darks."

He continues, "You will see the importance of the values within the colors and how they alone create the illusion of form. Plus you will learn to use the paint in new ways. You will also practice parallel and curved strokes." We also learn more about the shadows of objects we draw.

This entire week Esha and I go to class together. We have become close friends; we walk hand in hand and talk about almost anything and everything. I sense the closeness and the connection that is building our friendship even stronger. The way she looks at me makes me believe we will be together one day.

On Friday, we submit our homework from last weekend and Kabir sir gives us a new homework assignment. This time he gives us a postcard, a picture of a lily flower with a bunch of leaves to transform it into a painting. This time I offer to do homework together at my place. But Esha insists we do it at her house this time as well. I convince her to go to my place first, have lunch together, and then go to her house for homework.

At home, Mom serves us Gobi Aloo—cauliflower with potato curry—and moong dal—lentil soup—with chapatti. I am surprised to learn Esha never had moong dal before. She loves the creamy texture of dal. After lunch, Mom makes us fresh muttha—buttermilk—which is supposed to keep you hydrated during Mumbai's hot summer days.

Wiping my buttermilk mustache, I enter the kitchen to let Mom know that I will go to Esha's for our homework.

She quibbles, "Last week, you worked at her house. This week, why don't you both work here in your room; nobody will bother you girls."

I say, "Yes Mom, I offered the same. But she doesn't have a table top easel like I have. She cannot carry her big H-Frame easel. So . . ." I tilt my head sideways a little, shrug my shoulders, and give the expression of what can I do, I need to go.

I collect my painting stuff and whisk off with her. I leave our empty glasses in the kitchen sink.

"OK, don't be late for dinner," Mom's voice fades in the background as we both run out.

"OK, Mom," I shout back with a hope she can hear.

When we reach her house, we are surprised to see she has visitors. One of her cousins and her four-year-old son from Dombivali are visiting them. She cuddles that little cute boy as soon as we enter her house. Next hugging her cousin, she compliments, "Akka—elder sister—you are looking gorgeous. It looks like this boy is making you run around. You have lost a lot of weight." Immediately, the little one talks, "Mavashi—aunt, mom's sister—you know what? Dad says the same thing to Mommy."

Esha asks with a naughty cue, "What does Dad say?"

"Dad says, 'Mommy you are gorgeous'," he says with innocence on his face and in his voice dominating the words he utters. All of us chuckle. It leaves Akka blushing; that signals the couple is much in love. Esha bends down to babble with the little prince more. "What else does your dad say?"

We all give out a good laugh at her question. But the little boy, unaware of Esha's naughty intentions, says, "My dad always says my mommy has magic hugs. You know how? Her hugs make my boo-boo go away magically."

I find it cute. I don't want him to stop talking. But now Akka jumps in and asks him to watch TV. Esha then introduces me to Akka. The two of them catch up on a few of their relatives. Soon Esha takes a leave from her cousin and we carry on to her room. I offer to leave. She says no it's fine, I should stay. Her mom instructs us, "Please lock the room door before you start your painting, otherwise this naughty boy will make the whole room colorful."

Esha locks the room door. I settle my stuff on her table. She turns the AC on, saying, "It's hot in here today." I don't mind it because I am a little toasty too. The buttermilk we drank is not helping cool down the Mumbai heat.

When we finish applying primer on the hardboard, she stretches her arms yawning and says, "I am tired. Need to lie down for a while. Please wake me up in half an hour."

I nod almost staring her. She places one arm behind her neck as she lies down. Then she stretches her body bending one knee slightly outward.

"Oh boy," I splutter under my breath turning toward my hardboard to calm my racing heart. I can't focus after that. I turn around again to peek at her. She is fast asleep and has already pulled a blanket over her.

"Apparently the room's AC is working," I say to myself in disappointment.

I finish drawing flowers and leaves on the hardboard using Titanium White with the addition of thinner to make it flow easily and dry quickly.

After drawing, I am tired too. The room is getting cold. I see no other blanket there. I have no choice left. Subsequently I nudge her to move. I lie down next to her sharing the same blanket.

She opens a lazy eye, moves on the bed from one side to another and goes back to sleep. I slide on her bed, put on the shared blanket and close my eyes. Now her face is close to my bare neck. I can feel her breathe.

Keeping my eyes closed, I turn one side toward her and wrap my arm around her as if not to let her go, never ever. I love the way my arms touch her. An absurd desire to touch every inch of her is at the peak. Unaware of my own actions, I play a game with my fingers on her soft slender body. First I touch her forehead, then slowly her nose to her soft, perfectly shaped, beautiful lips. When I touch her lips, I feel a kiss on my one finger, then another. I try to get up. But she goes on kissing. She kisses all five fingers of my hand. I slightly rise from where I am sleeping, to look into her eyes. My palms are sweaty. My eyes meet hers. I see passion in her eyes, a desire to come close. The craving to touch her is intense, her eyes pleading to continue. I have no intention to stop either. I bring my face close to hers.

Abruptly there is a strong knock on the door. "Esha, Akka is leaving. Come bid goodbye to her," her mom says tapping the door from outside.

She jumps out of the bed to go out, leaving me alone with butterflies in my tummy. I follow her. We come out of the room and bid Akka goodbye. After the visitors leave, the house is somewhat silent. I get ready to leave too as clock ticks almost 8:00 in the night. Esha insists on her coming to drop me to my place. I smile. Her mom makes fun of us, "Esha you drop Soni to her house, then she can come to drop you and you both keep doing this the whole night." We giggle, gaze at each other and say, "Not a bad idea!" We all laugh.

Her mom then suggests I stay with Esha at their place for the night. As much as I want to, I know my mom won't allow. But, I promise her we will plan it soon.

In the moonlight, with many people around us rushing to their homes, we enjoy the walk. Her hand is holding mine gently, but firmly cupped. It's the best walk I ever had. I wish my house should have been a little farther away from hers. When we reach a parking lot just below my apartment building, after saying bye to her, I walk to the elevator. But this girl now is up to something else; she does not let go of my hand. The more I struggle to get my hand out of hers, the tighter she holds it. My cheeks turn red with nervousness. What if Girish sees us like this, what if a watchman sees us?

"It hurts when you hold it tight. Please let go of my hand," I request.

"I am not holding it tight, you are the one who doesn't want to leave," she says with a wry grin and releases my hand. We both chuckle. She gives a peck on my cheek and we wave bye to each other.

*****

Saturday morning

Mom comes down with an upset stomach, which interferes with my plan to go to a movie with Esha. I am sad and can't stop thinking about her. But Mom's health is important and besides there is no one else to take care of her. I call Esha to let her know about Mom's condition and cancelation of our movie plan. She becomes upset and says, "I miss you." I can imagine her tilting her head sideways, pouting her lips out and saying it. For a minute I forget that I have a sick mom to take care of. Mom hasn't had anything since morning except a few glasses of boiled water mixed with sugar and salt and her medicines.

By noon, Mom gets a little better. I grab the chance to call Esha again.

"I am happy that aunty is feeling better," she says.

"I miss you, Esha," I express.

"Awe . . . you do? Me too."

After taking a small pause, she hangs up the phone hastily saying, "OK, bye."

I have no clue of where this girl is flying. I go to the kitchen to cook khichadi—a mixed dish of rice and lentil cooked to a soft texture for easy digestion—for Mom. I have soaked rice and lentil in water since morning to make the khichadi softer and quicker. I place a pressure cooker on the stove. In ten to fifteen minutes, when the pressure cooker is about to blow its whistle, I hear the doorbell. I wonder who it is at this time of the day; it is hot and humid outside. I open the door to see Esha. Right then, pressure cooker's whistle blows. I run to turn the stove off. Esha rushes behind. Unexpectedly, she stops and then comes close to me. I step back a little to lean on the kitchen counter. She comes even closer, bringing her mouth near my ears, making my heart skip a tiny beat. Even after walking in hot weather, she sure looks as fresh and energetic as ever.

"Is aunty sleeping?" She backs off a little after whispering in my ear.

"S—she is," I fumble, and she breaks into titters.

"Look at you girl, you look damn nervous," she says.

I turn away from her, reaching for a plate to serve Mommy khichdi, I say, "Because, I thought . . ."

I am interrupted by her, putting her hand over my lips to tell me to be quiet. She stands close to me. I can feel the warmth of her breath. She wraps her arms around my shoulders, our eyes staring into each other's.

"Cupid's arrow has finally stricken me . . . boy what a feeling . . ." she sighs.

My stomach clenches. I put my arms around her waist. I am gasping, reducing the gap between us. I am nervous and excited at the same time. Surprisingly, otherwise chirpy girl, Esha looks extreme calm and confident, as if she knows exactly what will happen next, her eyes telling me, "Bring it on, I am all for it."

We kiss. Her lips on mine, our eyes closed. Her hands draw me closer to her face. I move my fingers through her hair. The plate from my other hand slips off with a loud echoing noise.

"Are you OK, Soni, Beta?" I hear Mom calling.

Esha pushes me away from her pointing me to go to Mom's room. Sometimes it's hard to predict what this girl wants and what she will do.

"Yes Mom," I gasp. I moan and walk away in disappointment. Esha follows behind with a plate of khichadi in her hands. Mom eats some of it. She doesn't want to nap anymore. She is concerned that if she sleeps any longer, she will be wide awake in the night like an owl. Nevertheless, I am glad she feels much better now.

*****

The next few weeks
In painting class we keep working more and more on using different colors, different forms, distance, and texture. This week, the end of the distance and texture class, the last concept of the entire painting class, and we don't get any homework. Instead we have to go to the studio on Saturday and Sunday, to finish the assignment. Everybody has to draw the picture of the ocean view that we see from the classroom window. Now I understand why the easels are set up in this way so we can paint the ocean. The view that we saw every day during our painting sessions, the view that we were engrossed by, unknowingly it became part of our lives. Now, that part of life, we have to bring into our art. This is Kabir sir's way of telling us to always look around you for new ideas and what you find will surprise you.

It is fun working in the studio six hours straight on a weekend. We all enjoy working on this assignment.

Kabir sir orders in lunch for us. We all gather to eat and chat. Other students in the class and their passion for painting amaze me. As unbelievable as it seems, these two days gave us lifetime friends too. One student, Laksh—meaning aim—like his name, is clear on how he will change painting from his hobby to his profession. He has plans on how he will turn it into his career.

It is unfortunate that Esha and my parents think of painting only as a hobby. Coming from a middle-class background, our parents consider having a practical career that earns enough to feed a family as a primary need. When our talks begin to turn into depressing conversations, Kabir sir quickly interrupts, "In your life, whenever any of you are ready to make painting as your career, please do let me know. I will be honored to help you and support you in whatever ways I can, no matter whether anyone else is supporting you or not. And, I really mean it." This leaves us all delighted. With that remark, Kabir sir takes us back to our assignments.

After many hours of hard work, our assignment is finally completed.

*****

Monday
When we come back to regular class, Kabir sir wants all of us to spend a day to review each other's ocean

view paintings. We remark with at least one positive note about the painting and one area of improvement. According to Kabir sir, an artist always benefits from constructive criticism to understand what to and what not to do while painting.

Among all us students, Laksh's and Esha's painting are the best. Esha's ocean view portrait looks lively as if it's the real ocean and not just a painting. On the other hand, Laksh's creation makes his ocean seem as if it is ready to come out of the boundaries of the hardboard, passionate and eager to move, to hit the bank of the ocean.

We all are sad since it's the last week of the class. I want to learn more from Kabir sir. I am not sure though when I will get that chance again in life, if at all. We all exchange numbers and emails in a hope to stay connected. I didn't realize where and how the last six weeks have flown by. We are lucky to have learned under the guidance of the great artist, Kabir sir. On the last day of the class, a thought that, going forward, Esha and I won't be able to spend much time together, chokes my throat. Tears make their way from my eyes to my cheeks. But Esha is optimistic. In her rationale, since we live close by, we can meet often. We can also go out to spend time together before our results are out and college starts. I couldn't agree more with her. I am amused at the way I am slowly turning into an emotional wreck from being the calm and composed Soni who two years back only hung out with a gang of boys' friends. They all loved me because they thought I was different from other girls who are more drama queens than a normal being. I think love has taken over me and is changing me a little every day. I don't even realize it unless incidents like today happen where I sink into my emotions and Esha stands out strong to bring me out of it. Her grip on my heart gets stronger day by day, hour by hour, every minute and every bit of each second.

CHAPTER 8. A LITTLE PLANNING, A LITTLE PRAYING

ONLY ONE MORE WEEK TO GO for our twelfth standard result. Esha and I plan, and lace it with prayers, to get into the same college, the same branch of engineering if possible. The fretfulness of the result dwells inside us. No tonic of humor, laughter, and positivity is able to subdue our anxiety at this point.

An evening before the result, we take a relaxing walk in a park opposite BNC Hospital in Mulund East to soothe our nervousness relating to the results. We hold hands and walk. Instead of enjoying each other's company, instead of having fun with each other, worry about the future makes us restless. Even though we walk in a slow and relax manner, we always get ahead of elderly people who are also taking a stroll in the park. While discussing about the results, Esha cries. When I ask the reason, wiping her tears, she says, "I am like that; whenever I am anxious and nervous about something, I can't stop crying." Instantly, she smiles and cries yet again. Then she mentions that she always weeps during exams thinking she won't do well and when the results come out, it's not bad at all. She has always been hard on herself when it comes to exams. She always has high expectations set for good results. This is a new side of her that I become aware of. Had I not experienced it now, I would have never believed this girl could whimper at all.

*****

My results are out today. Everybody at home is happy with my results but me. I scored 94.66% in the PCM (physics chemistry math) group, which is not that bad to get into a decent private engineering college. I am not sure if I will get in the same college and branch as her. Each 0.33% counts for admissions. Esha earned 95.33% in PCM. She is not worried at all. She tries to cheer me up. I am not as happy with my results, but I am delighted and thankful for something else. On this day, after many weeks, Girish talks to me nicely and wishes me luck. In excitement, I hug him and he embraces me back. That makes me think, perhaps now all is well between us. I reflect, possibly, he has forgiven me for what I said earlier on Esha that made him mad. He even volunteers to come to school with me next day to collect the paper copy of my results as his final exam preparation holidays are going on. Di and Jiju—brother-in-law—also come that evening for dinner to congratulate me.

This is my day, but as usual Di is Di, she can't stop boasting about herself, never ever . . . how could she not brag today? "See . . . I bought your favorite sweets, Pakiza—popular Bengali sweet—since you passed," she emphasizes with her chest expanding in pride, more for bringing sweets than for my results. Jiju completes her sentence, ". . . since you passed with such good marks, Soni. Very well earned, congratulations," he wishes, hugging me. As usual, I miss no chance of gulping my favorite sweet. I immediately grab one. It is fresh and soft. As soon as I put it in my mouth, it melts down. One is gone down fast enough that I see myself reaching out for another one. A sweet, especially Pakiza, is my favorite indulgence. If ever I win a lottery, unlike other girls, I won't go for clothes, jewelry, shoes, and purse shopping. Instead I would spend loads of money on eating and enjoying life.

After dinner, we all chat for long hours before going to bed. Next morning, Girish and I go to school, to collect the results. We talk to a few of the teachers who are there in school that day. It turns out to be a nice opportunity for him to see his old teachers. Overall we have a great time walking together in the school campus, greeting teachers and enjoying the compliments that we get from them. Almost every teacher repeats something in coherence, "You both, brother and sister, did well in your twelfth grade. Sonia, now you need to follow your brother's footsteps to get in a nice professional degree college."

My teachers know my interest is in Math, more than in Biology. Accordingly, they suggest currently hot and in-demand branches of engineering. But my criterion for engineering admission differs from all theirs. Mine is much simpler, I believe. I want to be in the same college and class as Esha.

Today, when I am with Girish in school, somehow I don't get worried at all about what if we see her, what if she comes and says hi or something else. I cherish these moments being with him and don't think about what ifs at all unlike other times.

When all the official work—collecting mark sheets, leaving certificate etc.—at school is done, he announces that he will take me for a treat to a cake shop for my favorite black forest pastry. I give him a high-five with a wide grin dominating my face.

"I have not been to that cake shop for many months now," I say. I couldn't think about going there without him. He loves black forest pastry as much as I do. How could I eat it without him and especially when he was not talking to me? I am beyond ecstatic to spend time with him like before. Just when I think, could life be any more perfect, something happens. As we reach the school's main gate to leave for Monginis cake shop, what Girish sees is enough for him to lose his cool and make me say, "Oh . . . shoot!"

Esha comes running in my direction leaving her mom to dawdle. She squeezes my hand and congratulates me, but I don't put my hands around hers. "Same to you," I say in a wry tone, praying she doesn't talk anymore and leaves right away.

A few months back, I had told Girish that I've decided to not to look at Esha again just because he meant more to me, more than anybody else. That is how his anger melted a little, though things had never got back to normal until yesterday. But I never shared with him that Esha and I have become great friends, during our painting class.

Here she is with all of her gregarious act which I think will surely put me in double trouble. I never told Esha about Girish and his family. Likewise I could not tell Girish about my friendship with her.

"By the way, who is he?" she asks in low voice winking at me, but not so low as not to be heard by him.

"We need to get going," I say, ignoring her question and moving my gaze from her to him, I continue, "Shall we?"

After this encounter, I know that I won't be able to get away with my behavior, and will have to face questions from both of them. The rest of the way to the pastry shop we both wear tightly zipped lips. I can sense the tension surrounding us. I can sense that he wants to ask something about her. After many months, he has talked to me as before. I don't want him to stop speaking to me again. Thankfully, his actions show he too feels the same way. After buying pastry, we sit on chairs, setting the pastry box in front of us on the table. Before taking a bite of it, he opens his securely fastened lips, and says, "I know, the last few months I have been harsh and rude in my behavior to you. I don't like that either. But when you see somebody who you love extremely, doing something wrong, it hurts," he says.

"There is no need for me to say this, but you know how much I trust you and care for you. I hope you don't break that trust," he inculcates.

"This is unexpected, calm words and warning at the same time. Today I am saved," I reply in a tone of ridicule.

"By the way, how do you know each other . . . so well?" he asks, raising his brows.

"Hey . . ."

He interrupts me, "No, seriously, I mean . . . she was like hugging you and all . . . and you never told me you knew her."

"I met her in the painting class I was going to this summer. She lives in Mulund too. We traveled together and we are friends now," I say, justifying my actions.

Then we talk more, mostly on random topics. Eventually, he reveals the secret that he is falling for a girl in his class. They both are great friends, and this guy is planning to ask her out soon. No wonder the love angel is the reason for his unexpected calm, even after the chance meeting we had with Esha.

I get it now, I muse.

After that for hours he keeps talking about his to be girlfriend. I don't miss a single chance to pull his leg. We both laugh together for hours over a piece of cake and chit chat. I am relieved to spend an awesome time with my best buddy.

*****

I am ready to get bombarded by Esha for my behavior at school when she saw me with Girish. As anticipated, the otherwise thrilled chatter box turns into an angry bird today and hits this poor girl, me that is, with her questions like pellets from a slingshot.

"Who was he, why did you ignore my question yesterday . . .?" blah blah blah.

Once I tell her he is my cousin, she flings more questions at me, complaining how I never told her about him and yesterday also why I didn't introduce them.

As always, she doesn't stay put until she is done with all her interrogations. Putting aside our celebration, I spend a good amount of time to answer her questions and explain my reasons behind not telling her about him. While talking about my fears, my fright of losing the best cousins' relationship, I almost weep. Instantly, she hugs me, saying, "Worry not, everything will be fine."

God knows where this girl gets this much positivity from. That is something, I want to get transferred from her into me. We both behave like silly kids whose tears ooze before every single act. The celebration to our success starts off with tears as I explain to her my fears of losing him. It also ends with both of us sniffling with doubts of not getting in the same college, let alone the same class. One more time, we discuss all our options to get into the same engineering college. Finally we both decide and agree on a college where Esha's dad is a member of the board of trustees. Our first option is Computer Science and our second choice is Electronics and Telecomm. We also choose other colleges in our list as the backup plan.

But all in vain; my dad doesn't agree on Electronics and Telecomm. He keeps saying, "Get into any decent engineering college of Mumbai, but only go with Computer Science."

Somehow Dad came to know that it takes years and years to settle down in the electronics side of the career, but it's comparatively easier to establish in the Computer Science line. That means, most likely, I will not get into the same college as her.

*****

Admission Day

Esha has her round of admission interview in the morning at 9:00 and I have mine at 11:30. I can't get into the same college as her and as a matter of fact any other college. In the admission committee, there is a fellow, Dad's college-time friend; he suggests to Dad that I skip getting into any college in this first round if he wants to get me in Computer Science, which is not available at the moment. He explains how many students block the seat at first and once they get into the medical school of their choice or something else, then they cancel this blocked seat. So here we go, we skip the first round of admission. The whole month between the first and second round, feels like years. I feel like being empty handed. Esha and I fight a lot during this month. She is annoyed at me knowing I have left electronics from the same college as her. I say nothing because she has a point there. Dad forced me to skip the round. I can't believe he did that; otherwise I would have gotten electronics in that college for sure. At least we would have ended up in the same college if not the same class. But no, Dad didn't even care what I wanted. I have never seen him take such a stubborn stand on anything related to me like this before.

*****

After many worrisome days and nights, today is my second round. With sweaty palms and heart that throbs like a horse's, I enter the admission room. When I enter the room, I pray under my breath, "I need to get into Computer Science in the same college as her. Please God, please," and move on to the first desk in admission hall. Finishing a couple of formalities at that desk, I move on to the next desk.

"Which branch, madam?" asks the man behind the desk.

"Computer Science," my dad replies.

"You are lucky madam, only one Computer Science seat is available," he says enthusiastically. The glow on his face is of some kind of victory as if he is getting admission and not me.

Dad is excited. Even without knowing the college he adds, "Yes, we want it."

Even before I can understand anything, we are moved to the next desk all the way through to the end, till all the paperwork is completed. I become more and more anxious to know the college I will go to. Before we leave from the admission room, Dad wants to thank his friend for his suggestion on skipping the first round.

I think, *Thank him? For what? I was lucky to get that last seat of Computer Science. What if I wouldn't have gotten it, what if I would have ended up with nothing or something in a college that I never heard of?*

"Oh . . . wait a minute; I still don't know the college I will go to. It is quite possible that I am going to some random college I really don't know about," I say. A cascade of questions is running through my brain.

My dad's friend takes a break from his duty and joins us on our way out from the admission room. First, he congratulates me. I reply with a wry smile and say "Thank you" in an unhappy voice. Then he puts his hand around my dad's shoulder, congratulating him. "Oye Arora, it's not easy to get admission to Thadomal Computer Science with her percentage."

I can't believe my ears, "Which college?"

"You got into Thadomal, no? That is what I am saying," he replies back.

"Oh . . . yes, yes," I say casually, as if I knew about it already. But secretly, I become excited to know that I will go to the same college and class as her. My heart does a happy somersault.

"I know all the statistics of admissions for the second round, from my experience of years of working in the admission committee," he boasts with pride. "I don't tell that to everybody, but you are my buddy. Let's go to the canteen and you buy me Samosa and tea," he continues, bringing his arm down that was resting on Dad's shoulder all this time. While savoring samosa and tea, Dad and his friend refresh their college time memories. From their conversation, I gather Dad had a great deal of fun in those days and he used to be hilarious and jovial. I guess he has lost that side of him over his responsibilities.

I call Esha as soon as I reach home. I pretend to be sad and refuse to share anything regarding my admission over the phone. I even pretend a sniffle over the phone and then hang up after deciding the time and place to meet her in the evening. I am super excited to play this prank on her. I imagine it would be hilarious to see this bubbly girl, being sad, just for fun.

As decided, I reach Prashant fast food near the station. I wait for ten to fifteen minutes before she shows up. As usual, she is cheerful today. I fake a sad face and even don't reveal any excitement on seeing her.

"What's the matter Soni? What happened?" she asks mischievously.

I maintain the silence to create more effect.

"Speak, will you? Otherwise how will I know what happened?" she pushes assertively.

"I wish Dad wouldn't have forced me to skip the first round of admission. At least we would have ended up in the same college," I express, keeping my gaze on the table, as if I am upset.

"What are you saying?" she demands with a raised voice. All the people sitting in the restaurant turn to look at us. Seeing this, she lowers her voice. "OK . . . ok. Tell me everything. You know I don't like suspense. I want all the details." She sounds a bit irritated.

Nice . . . seems the prank is working, I can't believe it and continue pretending to be in a sad mood. I tell her the whole story, of course not the real one. I crane forward, place my hands on the table and cup my face between my palms. Adding to the effect of my forged mood, lowering my lower lip, I tell her that I am going to VJTI.

Immediately, she leans forward from across the table and consoles me, touching my cheeks, to cheer me up. "Don't worry, we will still see each other every evening after coming home from college. Cheer up now."

I get slightly furious. I think, *what the heck! This girl is not getting mad at all. How come?*

I spice up my acting with a bit of rage, "What is this yaar—dude? I am sad that we won't be going to the same college and look at you. You are still behaving as if nothing is wrong. How could you, Miss Optimistic?" I toss at her, followed by silence for a few seconds.

She is still quiet. I am miffed and give up. Then I say, "Dang it, my prank didn't work." I say

All of a sudden she starts laughing. "I knew it, girl, and I tricked you nicely," she says, winking at me.

I refuse to talk for a while because I couldn't play a prank on her successfully. Or perhaps because I was disappointed that she didn't believe me. But again one can't be upset for a long time when she is around. I smile at her; in return she shares the reason behind her coming late. She talked to my mom once I left. There it is, now I know, Mom spilled the beans.

CHAPTER 9. GOOD TIMES

THE FIRST DAY OF COLLEGE is finally here. Our hearts beat faster and louder with a little nervousness and a lot of excitement. Any ragging is banned by law, but many seniors use the term introduction pretty loosely. Under the name of introduction, they ask us to do some—so-called fun—activities, though we think it is mental torture and harassment. The first day we both escape meeting any seniors.

The next day, a group of second-year girls comes in and asks a few of us to walk with them to the canteen.

"No reason to be scared of anything. OK?" states one of them softly.

"Don't be scared. We will not eat you...." roars one with big and scary eyes, followed by a long laugh, ". .

. unless you don't do what you are asked to do, ha ha ha ha . . ."

All the other girls join her in the laughter; it seems like she is the queen bee. The insanity relating to all this introduction drama is, these seniors crack jokes in front of us and we may not smile. If they catch any of us smiling or laughing, that fresher will be assigned a tougher task to do, tougher mentally than physically. Guess how would we know this and many other funky rules? Nobody tells us. Those rules are announced on the fly as and when any of them pleases. I am the first one to be honored with this punishment not because I laughed, but because I denied doing the first act, they gave me. Didn't I tell you that nobody tells us about those rules beforehand?

As soon as we reach the canteen, they ask me to propose to a senior guy. How could I do that? Never in my dreams, have I imagined we will do all this nonsense in engineering college. I am taken to this senior guy by one of the senior bees. She commands, "Now imagine, he is the most handsome boy you have ever seen in your entire life and you want to marry him. Propose to him now." I don't say a word for roughly ten minutes.

Even before I can start the daunting task that is given to me, one other bee jumps in. "Keep your paws off him. He is mine," she shouts, looking in my eyes.

Immediately following, another senior bee's voice rises, "Propose to him . . . now."

Slowly most of the bees and the boy, I have to propose to, surround me. Every bee in that group orders me in a different way to do the act. When they create a task for you, half of them ask you to do it one way and other half say don't do it. What are we poor freshers supposed to do? One of them comes close and advises in a low voice right in my ear, "Just do it, doesn't matter what you say. Finish it, you will be saved."

I retort, "But I can't."

The impatient Queen Bee jumps in, this time with more attitude than the last time, with arrogance in her words and the way she stares at me. Even though I don't look at her to recognize the impertinence in her stare, somehow I can sense it. She says bluntly, "OK, fine. If you don't want to propose to this handsome guy, you have to propose to one girl here. Either you pick one or you will find out the drill."

By this time, beads of sweat have made their way from each junior's armpit to their shirts, showing wet patches. The tension during this so-called introduction is rising. I want to get this moment over with as fast as possible. That means I have to propose to one girl quicker, but I can't do that either.

The Queen Bee continues to talk after a few seconds of silence, "Maharaniji—Your Highness the Queen—have you yet decided to whom you want to propose?"

Giving no one else a chance to speak, she presses on, "Please come Maharaniji, come this way and ask this girl if she will marry you," she says and points me to Esha.

Oh boy . . . why is this happening? is the first thought that comes to my mind when I gaze at Esha's face, which turns all pink, maybe due to rise in adrenaline because of uneasiness for what is going on. I can sense how scared she is. And on top of that now we both are on the spot. At that instant, I regret not having done the very first task. I shouldn't have denied proposing to the boy to begin with.

Please do it now, never too late, I persuade myself and take a step toward her. No doubt that Esha is the girl who I would like to ask this that I will ask her right now, but definitely not this way. I close my eyes, embarrassed. I cannot take the risk to refuse the task once again and bear one more punishment.

Someone nudges me in my arm.

"Take this flower. Move on, go propose to her," a senior blurts picking a flower from the bin and handing it to me.

"What's your name?" another bee questions Esha.

"Esha!" comes her quiet reply. She sounds as embarrassed as me.

"Speak! Go ahead with your proposal now," demands another senior.

The group has now encircled us; silence is in the air. I pick the flower, hold it in front of Esha. I look at her. She is still staring at the ground, beads of sweat trickling down her face. She is quiet.

"Life is love. Love is you."

"Esha, I love you from the bottom of my heart and promise to do anything to make you happy," I stammer and abruptly I hear a big chuckle from the seniors surrounding us. I hear many comments making fun of me.

Without getting bothered by their remarks, I continue.

"I can't imagine another day of my life without you. I promise to be by you till the end."

"The world seems a magical place whenever I think about you, dream about you. Would you like to make my world even more magical? Will you marry me?"

By now, Esha looks in my eyes and a thin smile dawns on her face.

Half a minute passes by in a pin-drop silence.

Suddenly, the queen bee shrieks at Esha, "Your turn now lady. Reply back."

All the seniors surrounding us laugh, "Yes yes, you have to accept her proposal."

"Huh! Yes. Yes, I will marry you," Esha says, with naughtiness in her eyes that only I notice.

Queen Bee, mockingly, gives a brief hug to both of us to congratulate and asks, raising one of her brows, "On what date do you both want to get married? We need to print the wedding cards." All the bees laugh and with clenched teeth, I breathe heavily. It is surely humiliating the way we are asked to do the task in the name of introduction.

Looking at her other friend, one bee asks, "Do we even know the names of these girls to print on the card?" followed by a chuckle. To avoid the worst, we oppose nothing that they ask us to do now. One time punishment on task denial was enough to learn a lesson. Hence, we both tell our names, first I say out my name loud and clear, followed by her.

I have to agree that Queen Bee is spontaneous in her thoughts and things she says for teasing anyone. Within a fraction of seconds, as soon as Esha and I are done saying our names out loud, Queen Bee asks, "Sonisha, have you both decided the date yet or not?"

When every other bee gives Queen Bee a questioning expression about her name calling, she makes it clear, "Sonisha (Sonia + Esha) is the new name for this couple from now on." They even decide the pretend wedding date for us. After that they call it a day for ragging.

Thankfully, the day is over. I couldn't believe all that was going on. While returning home, we both hope that this drama doesn't continue like the seniors mentioned, wedding cards and all that. Today was embarrassing as is. Nevertheless, we both like the name Sonisha.

*****

A few months slip by. Our first semester exam approaches faster than we thought. We worry for our exam that will start in fifteen days.

"What, only fifteen days? OMG, how are we going to finish all the preparations?" Esha gets all anxious when I remind her about our exam schedule. *Crying and exam anxiety, not again*, I say in my mind when I see her all restless.

We study together, at her place, every evening after coming home from college and weekends too. We religiously follow the schedule and yes, we study☺.

A weekend before my exam starts, Di comes to stay with us since she doesn't feel well. She needs rest.

There is no other better place than Mum's to get the tranquility that is what she would say. And I can't deny that. Saturday morning before leaving for work, Jiju drops her off. We all have breakfast together, then Jiju leaves. After chatting with Di, when I stand up to go to Esha's house for studies, Di asks, "Is this the same girl who you proposed to in college?"

"How do you know, Di?"

"If you don't tell me what you think, I won't find out," she asserts with disdain.

After a few seconds of pause, she continues, "You know Shikha in your class, she lives in our building. She told me everything."

Once Di starts, there isn't any stopping her. *But I better get going*, I think.

"You know that was all part of our ragging," I reply casually going toward the room to grab my backpack. I walk out of the room with my bag and Mom walks out of the kitchen going toward the dining area. As usual, Di doesn't miss the perfect timing to poke me while Mom is around.

"I know it's not only about ragging. Shikha told me how you both are always together and all." Usually I give in to what Di says to avoid an argument. Anyways, I can't win an argument against her. But this time, I feel I am getting ready to stand up for myself, which is unusual from what I used to do. I turn back to stare at her and frown, "So, what are you trying to say? Say it clear and direct."

It is the first time I ever got mad at my Hitler sister. She realizes my anger is ready to jump out. Avoiding me, she turns to Mom and emits in fury, "Mom, I am telling you. You need to keep an eye on her. She is not behaving as a good kid in college."

Mom smiles and tells her, "Don't worry, Pahal. Our Soni won't do anything wrong. Just relax. You need to take care of yourself. Ease down."

I walk out of the house like manic, pondering, *whatever Di said was 100% right, but what I didn't understand is why was I annoyed at her. It could be I expected that nobody in college would know about us being this close. After all, we act the same as any other two best friends, may it be Renu-Richa or Prachi-Sana. Why the hell would Shikha say anything wrong about us? On top of that, Di is like the BBC. She can keep nothing to herself. I have many secrets of hers that I never let out, not even to Girish. But she is impossible!*

When I share my agitation with Esha, she places her hand on my shoulder and says, "Chilax babe. You know what," followed by a short gap in a cinematic way. I raise a brow as if to ask what. "You love your sister a lot. Even though she doesn't realize that, you expect the same from her as you do for her . . .

meaning keeping secrets . . . ha ha ha," she finishes and laughs out loud.

"Come on Esha, I am tense here and you are making fun of me and my problem, instead of helping me out," I yell at her.

She immediately goes into soft mode. "Soni, I was just joking to lighten your mood. Don't worry about Di and all other crap right now. The need of the hour is to concentrate on our studies and exams," she says, giving me a sisterly hug.

Our exam is only a few hours away. Right now we need to concentrate on that. But I am sure our—Esha and my—life together will not be less than an exam. Thoughts about Di's comments dance in my head for a few hours. But I have no other choice than to concentrate on my studies at this moment. Never in my school life have I studied as hard as I am cramming this year. Perhaps it is Esha's magic. I feel a strong desire to achieve something, the desire to present my best when she is around me, with me. But at the same time I get scared wondering will we be always together. This fright lurches my stomach. It doesn't let me breathe and spills the tears out of my eyes. Many times I wonder if she has the same worries as me, whether we'll be together forever or not. Whenever I ask her, she always responds in her naughty way, "Worry not dear. Where would I go without you?"

*****

We both do well in exams. After coming out of the exam hall, we discuss our answers and mock the professors until we reach home. Esha's crying episodes before exams are both horrible and funny all at the same time. At times, it's difficult to stop her from sobbing. I never imagined a girl with her level of positive attitude otherwise could weep this much just from exam anxiety. *Instead of being prey to nervousness why doesn't she handle it with self-belief and faith in herself?* I contemplate. Sometimes I believe I know her well. As soon as I think that, the next moment another side of her personality, something that was hidden before, comes out. And I am left with a big aha moment. She can be the life and soul of the party or she can be like the gentle butterfly who can get hurt easily or she can be like a kid with a soft heart who can't stand any uncertainties in her life.

When I visualize the scene of just before entering the exam hall, a gentle smile touches my face. On one side is Esha's crying episodes, on the other side our classmate Rohan eating everybody's brain to revise the syllabus. I can never imagine how somebody can revise a whole year of the syllabus in just half an hour. And the group of five girls, who are mockingly known as the "Nerd Beauties," can't stop babbling about what they have learnt and memorized. Till the last minute before the exam starts, they keep discussing questions, theories, and formulas. Then there is the "Gang of Cool Dudes"—that is how the group of four boys likes to be addressed—they never study. According to the statements they boasted of, whatever they have learnt in class and revised before the last few hours of the exams, will promote them to the next class. They are cool with that. They say, "We Cool Dudes are cool with that." Esha always makes fun of them saying yes we recognize you are C-O-O-L (Constipated – Overweight – Out of style – Losers)

Based on who studied how much or who is sharp, everybody gets paid back accordingly, in terms of term results. I secure second place and Esha secures third, amidst all the first year students of our college. My family, especially Dad is thrilled with my results. He takes the whole family for dinner to Delish Relish as a treat for my results. I have heard a lot about it since Dad and Mom went there once with their friends. Of course, Di had been there too with Jiju. Girish too went there a few times with his medico friends. I am the only one in the family who has never been there. I am excited to go, I can't wait.

Delish Relish is the hawker's—a vendor of food—restaurant, right behind the Taj Hotel. Di and Jiju will join us too. Girish can't come since he has to study for his final exams that are approaching soon. I ask Dad if Esha can join us as well. He is fine with it. That place opens at 11:00 PM in the night. We plan to leave around 9:30 PM. As per the plan, Dad and I pick up Esha a little before we leave. When we go to pick up Esha, Dad requests her parents to let Esha stay with us tonight since he knows we will return late. They agree.

While we were gone to pick her up, Di and Jiju came home. I don't like Di's stroppy facial expressions when I introduce Esha to her and Jiju. Ignoring her ill manners, I let my excitement, to go to Delish Relish, float. I have heard a lot about the food they serve. I am literally jumping up and down. While we wait for the local train, Esha and Mom are talking; Di takes me aside and asks, "Why the hell is that girl coming with us? I thought it's a family dinner thingy."

"Come on, Di, she is my friend. She did well too in her exams. I wanted her to join us. Dad agreed. No big deal," I rejoin.

She gives me that typical Di's *I am watching you* stare.

She thinks way too much about us. I simply ignore her on this topic. I have never been out this late in the night, that too on the streets, where it's difficult to walk even at this hour of the night, 11:00 o'clock it is. Surprisingly, this street behind the Taj Hotel is equally lively and full of people as any other time of the day. The noise of cars honking and people blabbering is loud. I absolutely love it. Finally we enter the lane. The whole street is fully packed with people, some eating, some walking holding hands of their loved ones, some exchanging sweet nothings. I could see people from different circles of life as if life itself has arrived to celebrate all its colors right there on that small street. From beggars to people wearing branded watches, middle-class people like us too. People of all ages, groups of college students to groups of spoiled kids of rich parents, just married couples and families like us. A very narrow lane. A few cars parked on one side of the lane make it seem even narrower. On the other side of the road, tables and chairs are arranged for customers to sit and eat. Serving and eating, all is done under the streetlight as the sky plays the roof of this restaurant. It is a vibrant feeling being on this rowdy street just to eat delicious spicy food. The cocktail aroma of freshly cooked pav-bhaji, bhuna chicken, and mutton biryani makes me drool. I can't wait for my food to arrive. I look around at the other people while waiting for my food and hearing Di's non-stop chatter. Everybody seems to enjoy every bit of their food. I can't decide though if people are relishing the food more or adoring the presence of their loved ones.

Finally, our wait is over and our food is served at the table. Before we realize it, the food has gone into our tummies leaving a great deal of contentment and happiness on our faces. Even though we all are full, if we would have ordered more, it would have been finished.

I absolutely loved their mutton keema—*minced goat curry*. Everything about that place is different—the food, the sitting arrangements, timings—undeniably everything. It is an amazing experience. Esha and I have already made plans to come back again, but only the two of us. When and how? We don't know yet. The taste of that food will linger in my mind forever.

By the time we reach home its way past midnight. We both are eager about the sleepover since it means a whole night of talking and chitchatting— the favorite thing that girls like to do during a sleepover. A few times, when I went to her house, in the past, for sleepover, her mom would wake up in the middle of the night, knock on our door and say, "Girls, you need to go to bed now. It's very late. No more chatter and giggles please." That is when we would stop our conversations and doze off within no time.

"Wow, Soni that is such a sweet picture of your Di and you," she says sitting on the bed and picking up the photo frame I keep by my bedside.

She has been in my room once before, but that was for such a brief moment. This is the first time she is here for a sleepover. As a result she is super excited. We gab about our school days and how we didn't know each other even being in the same school for many years. Then in a rush, I share about my secret crush on her. That makes her blush. I see her cheeks turn red and my smile outlasts the whole conversation. We then continue talking about the boys and girls of our school. We make fun of some of our batch mates; mimic a few teachers, followed by a review of our last four years' yearbooks, one after another, comparing one to the other. We look at our own pictures from the four-year-old yearbook. We can't stop laughing to see how we looked then. We also gaze at Girish's picture. Comparing his picture from the four years older yearbook to the three years older yearbook, he looked entirely different in those two pictures. In one picture, he looks like a cute and innocent boy who can melt everyone's heart. Then in the next year's picture, he looks like he is growing into a man. He wears a visibly noticeable mustache with facial skin that is hardening a bit. While growing up with him, I didn't notice the small changes over the years. Maybe because I saw him every day. Every day's tiny change seemed natural. But now, looking at old pictures, I realize the difference. Reminiscing over old memories gives me a fussy feeling. Our talk takes many turns from school memories to scary stories, personal experiences to future plans. By now we are hungry again. I can't believe all that big portion of food we ate at Delish Relish, is already digested leaving us starving.

I tiptoe to the kitchen to get snacks to munch on. Stainless steel canisters are placed in the cabinet under a kitchen counter top. I open one canister carefully and slowly to avoid any noise. I take out two chips packets and hide-&-seek cream cookies. I try to hold two chips packet and a cookie pack in one hand while the other hand is closing the canister lid without creating much noise. 'Boom!'

No matter how careful I am, I drop the canister lid, waking up my mom. In a rush, I drop the chips and cookie packs as well. Then I close the lid. I smile at Mom to avoid any questions and go back to my room with my goodies as quickly as I can. Mom also goes back to bed after using the bathroom. We savor our early morning snack. I get tired and sleepy. But Esha's chatter can go on for the entire night without a single yawn. To accompany her a little longer, I wash my face and splash water on my eyes. But to no avail. Then I open the room windows to let fresh air in to take away my sleepiness. But after that, I don't remember when I doze off.

*****

The next day doesn't come as a lazy Sunday like we had thought. Instead, we both are enthusiastic to work on a painting. Most of the afternoon we spend on an acrylic portrait together that we have been planning for a long time, but haven't been able to do because of the exams schedule. We both desired to make a painting of two beautiful mermaids, who are best friends forever, like us. Most of it is Esha's idea. I could envision her becoming a superb artist. The way the painting turns out, we both are ecstatic.

I wish someday, her aspiration to have her own art gallery comes true. I want to be her partner in an art gallery since we both make an awesome team together. Mom's jaw drops in awe when she sees our painting. She cuddles both of us for our good work and gives us blessings, "Beta, my blessings are always with you girls. Keep up the good work." Her eyes express that she is very proud of us.

Late afternoon, we spend time lounging on the sofa and watching TV. Mom makes us nice, warm coffee. I show her my pictures from 8th–9th grade. She likes my tomboyish semblance in those pictures. Then my mom brings an old album, to show it to Esha, which has a few of Di's, Girish's, and my childhood memories. Esha laughs her heart out while looking at those pictures, especially mine. She finds it funny that in every single picture I was trying to copy Girish's pose. I am like, whatever! Like everybody else, she also comments, "Di looked neat even as a kid." She has a good time hearing our juvenile stories from Mom. I wish she could stay even longer. But she has to leave.

"Esha seems to be really nice girl," Mom articulates after she leaves. I don't know why, but it feels good to hear those words from my mom.

Chapter 10. A forever
LINGERING INCIDENT

One week later
Monday
ONE OF OUR CLASSMATES BREAKS the news to
us. Like every year, this year too our college faculty
plans a three-day trip to Mahabaleshwar for first-
year students. One class later, our physics teacher
Mrs. Navandar gives us the details about the outing.
We have a two weeks' time frame to reserve the spot
for ourselves. The entire class is excited to hear the
news. The rest of the day, during every break, all
students discuss about the tour. Everyone has lots of
questions contending in their head. Whether we will
get permissions from parents to go to trip? Can we
afford it? And many more.

Esha is pumped up too. She jumps up and down like
a kid to go on the trip. She always adds her zing to

everything she does. Jumping is one more example of that. Looking at my dull expressions, she shakes me holding my left arm. Acting dramatic, she asks me, "Why are you sad my girlfriend. Don't you wanna go with me? Tell, tell."

I don't want to burst her bubble, especially when she is happy about it. I get away from her question with a nice smile. A smile is the perfect answer to all those questions that one doesn't want to answer, I think in my head. I prefer to be quiet for the time being and will talk to her later regarding the trip. I can't pay attention in the next class; I keep contemplating about whether I will go, whether Dad will allow me to or not. In the house where we are not permitted to stay out after 10:00 PM without parents, how can I imagine getting away for three days and two nights, on a college trip?

"I am watching you since the trip news broke. What is bothering you about it, Soni?" she asks me while on our way to the station from college.

"I really want to go for this trip." I say with a wry smile.

"Exactly, I want the same," she adds, "but what is holding you back then?"

"I am not sure if Dad will allow me to go. He never lets us be out of the house late in the night, now getting away for a two-night college trip. I am not at all optimistic," I reply, shifting my gaze from her to the front, in the direction we are walking. The steps I am taking to move forward feel heavy as if I already know Dad's decision and its ramifications—something that has not really happened yet—but is already dwelling in me.

"Hmm . . ." she muses as if she is planning something in her head.

We keep moving without talking till we reach the station. All of a sudden, she turns to me. Keeping her one hand on my shoulder she commands in a confident voice, "You try to convince him. If that doesn't work, I have a great Plan B. We will discuss it when needed. Meanwhile, you do your part to convince your parents."

I shrug my shoulders and give a forced smile followed by a lower lip twitch, as if to say, "Whatever you say madam."

I know, convincing Dad will not be easy, especially after Di's news of being in a place where drugs were sold and all that. Yes, it annoys me. But whenever I want permission for anything that is against our house's norm, Di's incident is the first excuse that my parents bring up to say no. Most of the time, I find my way around by coaxing them, but this time I don't know how I can do that. I consider talking to Mom first, even though I know her response, like every time. But then I change my mind. I get Girish involved.

When he comes back from college, I go to him. He is sitting at the dining table, enjoying his evening snack of an apple. Aunty is cutting vegetables in the kitchen to prepare for dinner. I sit in a dining chair across from him. He picks another apple from the fruit basket kept next to him and throws it at me with a wide grin, "Eat and enjoy . . ."

I am not in the spirit to reply to him, so, catching the apple, I say coldly, "I am not in a mood for your jokes. I need your help with something."

He narrows his grin, sits tall, and says, "Yes, sister, at your service."

I tell him about my trip. "Most of my classmates are going. I want to go too. But you know Mom and Dad. I am afraid that they won't allow me, as usual," I say with disappointment drooping in my voice. I ask if he could back me up in front of my parents just in case they say no. "Definitely, I can do that. Just let me know when?" he affirms. He is still sitting tall as if trying to be serious to match my mood. I thank him.

"Hmm . . ." he continues, craning forward, keeping his hands on the dining table, "Let alone, backing you up, I can convince your parents to send you to the trip, but only if . . . only if you promise me one thing." He pauses for a moment.

"Yes, yes, whatever," I reply, fast forwarding that part of the conversation.

He adds, "No, no. Not whatever. Promise me, you won't do anything to ruin your parents' name. Don't get too close to anyone. You know what I mean," he says and winks at me. My prompt reaction, an apple throw that doesn't work as expected and lands on the ground. This boy for sure knows how to lift up my mood.

*****

I want to talk to Mom about my trip before Dad's arrival at home and have her on my team. As decided, Girish comes, touches mom's feet—the usual ritual that he performs when he meets my parents first time on any given day. In return, Mom gives him blessings, "Always stay happy and live in prosperity," followed by a hug. Now I am used to this ritual to an extent that many times it plays in my mind as soon as Girish enters the house. I almost blurted the blessing line, having heard the repetition a gazillion times. But thankfully, I hold my tongue tight in my mouth instead of uttering those words. My tongue and throat hurt from it. And then he asks about her day. He deliberately inquires about my day also in front of Mom. In response, I excitedly share with him about my college trip. He acts curious to hear more, everything as planned. Then, in a jiffy, I ask Mom if I can go. She is all no for it as anticipated.

She is cutting vegetables. I go close to her, take the knife out of her hand and set it on the kitchen counter top. I embrace her, and try to convince her saying, "It will be fun. All my classmates are going too." She is not ready to say yes. Girish jumps in the conversation, "Aunty, let her go. It is always great to go with the classmates. Teachers are always with them too. When I went for my class trip last year, you remember I told you guys, it was refreshing. After coming back from the trip, I felt revived and that helped me to study harder. I think you should allow her to have this experience."

A few seconds' silence. We wait for Mom to say yes. When Mom says nothing for a few seconds, Girish continues. "It is the best time to connect with classmates and to build new bonds. It will really help her during her third and fourth years' semester projects. Only from these friendships will they form their project teams."

Wow! I exclaim in my mind. He is doing an awesome job of putting facts in front of Mom. I didn't even think he will go this far.

Under the increasing insistence, from me and him, she replies back, "Beta, I have no problem. If she wants to go, she has my permission. But you know your uncle, he won't agree." That is the typical Mom response, even though she is the one who opposes many things, using Di's incident as an excuse.

He speaks again, looking at me, "Soni, you have aunty's permission. No worries, we will talk to uncle once he is home." Then, shifting his gaze to Mom, he probes, "We will convince uncle, right aunty?" as if to leave aunty with the job to convince uncle.

"OK, I will be back once uncle is here. I got to study now," he says.

I convey to him with my lip movement, while Mom gets back to cutting vegetables, *You are awesome!!!*

He leaves with a promise to be back soon. I again hug Mom, thank her and I add, "Mom, I want to help you in the kitchen today. What can I do?"

"Soni wants to help me in the kitchen; that is something unusual during school/college semester," Mom says with her attention still on cutting vegetables. When I don't unwrap my arms from around her, she demands, pushing me toward my room. "No need to flatter me anymore. Go and study."

We both get back to our respective work with a big chuckle.

Sharp at 9:00, dad arrives home. I can't control myself enough to postpone asking his permission for the trip. But I have to wait for Girish to show up. I keep myself rooted to my room with a book—which I do not pay attention to any more. Time ticks slowly. Mom knocks on my room door. "Dinner is ready and Dad is here too."

"Stupid Girish, why is he not here yet," I mutter.

"What did you say? Come fast," Mom demands.

"Nothing."

I open the door to walk out to his house. He is engrossed in his studies. Thus, he forgot about the time. "Sorry, sorry, let's go now," he says, reading my expression, and leads me to my house.

When we reach home, Dad is talking on the phone. "It's Di," Mom says, seeing the anxious look on my face. Mom serves food on our plates.

"Pahal's mom, you should cook Girish's favorite dal—lentil—more often that way we get to see him a little more," Dad expresses, looking at Mom first followed by Girish.

All of a sudden everybody is quiet. I can hear the clinking of spoons against plates. Usually at dinner table, Dad talks more. Today, his silence gives me a warning sign, "Wrong timing, no talking please." But, unable to hold my excitement and nervousness, I still jump in, "Dad, our college has organized a trip for all first year students."

Finishing the food bite that he has in his mouth, not moving the gaze away from the plate he nods and says indifferently, as if to hide something underneath his words, "Yeah, I know. Your Di told me."

Girish and I look at Mom as if she told Di about the trip. In return, she wobbles her head to gesture *not me, I don't know, who did.*

"All my classmates are going. This will be the good opportunity to build new friendships, connect with classmates. It would help to form teams for assignment discussions," I say, putting forward all the points that Girish mentioned earlier to Mom. I say it all assertively. Then I pause for his response. When he doesn't speak up, I insist on getting his affirmation, "I want to go, Dad, please."

"Is your friend Esha coming too? Di was saying something about . . . that she heard from her neighbor—your classmate," he says hesitantly.

Oh no, Di doesn't leave a single chance to ruin anything in my life, I cry under my breath.

"Dad, that was just a part of ragging, you know."

Kind of sensing the situation, even without knowing the complete story behind what Dad said, Girish pitches in, "Yes, I know. Uncle, in our college too we had much ragging. After the ragging is finished, there is nothing to worry about. The college trip is always fun. I think Soni should go. What do you say, aunty?"

"Oh yes, she should go. And her friend Esha is going too," mom replies being oblivious to the ragging incident. *Mom tried to help. But why does she have to bring up Esha's name?* I think.

"Let me think," Dad replies calmly, without a hitch. That reply worries me. It seems even harder to convince him than I thought. If it would have been studies related or painting related, he would have agreed easily without giving any second thought.

*****

After Girish leaves, Dad asks me to sit next to him on the sofa. He places his hand on my head, as if to give blessings, and then he says, "I hope you understand my concern. I am not yet ready again to take any risk when it comes to Pahal or you. One time was enough."

"I want to go, please," I plead. "I understand your concern, Dad. But, please give me one chance. I promise, I won't break your trust. I have always lived up to your and Mom's expectations. This time also, it won't be any different." I talk gingerly holding back all my grudges for Di. He is not ready to move a bit away from his decision. "I will call you and Mom every day. I promise I will behave as a responsible person as I always do. Big no to any stupid things. Please, Dad, let me go," I implore. In spite of trying hard, I can't convince him, so I burst into tears.

"Mom, Dad, this is done. I am tired. You guys can't hold on to Di's mistakes against me. Just because Di makes stupid mistakes, why should I always suffer? That is not fair to me. Moreover, she is married now for God's sake," I yell and walk away to the kitchen to stand at the window, staring outside. I try to calm myself. I concentrate on my breathing to relax, but nothing helps. I remember that Thursday evening when Di had landed herself in trouble.

That one Thursday evening, and the trouble that Di landed herself into, is still lingering over our house. That day, after dinner, at around 9:00 PM, Mom almost finished watching the famous Hindi TV Soap Opera, Kasauti Jindagi ki, which aired on the STAR Plus channel. As usual, Dad commented, "If you are done watching that useless drama, can I have a turn now for news, please."

Irritated, Mom handed over the remote to him. "I never get time from cooking, doing your laundry, and household things, to watch TV at all. I only watch this one serial and that too is mixed with your nagging. Here, take this remote, your TV, and go watch your news; as if these news people will pay you lacs of rupees to watch their channel." And then she walked away from the living room. Mom moving away with anger didn't impact Dad's decision to watch the news. Next I heard Dad screaming, "What the hell are they showing on TV? How is Pahal related to this drug news? Why is she on this news? Didn't she go to her friend's house to study? Would anyone tell me where is Pahal?"

Mom started walking and talking from her room to the TV room with a high voltage temper, "What is your problem? I am letting you watch new . . ." She gulped the 's' of the word news as soon as she saw what dad was watching on TV. After that she did not spit a single word till Di came home. Dad tried calling her friend's cell, but it was switched off. After watching the news and unable to get hold of her for the next hour and a half, our house was moaning, especially Mom, as in why had she agreed on sending Di to Bandra College. But Dad looked calmer compared to an hour and a half ago.

At around 10:30 PM, our doorbell rang. Here came Di and there went Mom's word fire. "This is what you do in the name of studying with your friend. We gave you liberty and this is what you give us back. You keep calling him your friend; I am doubtful now. Anyways, you lied to us. God knows how many other lies you have given to us. What would people say when they watch it? Who would marry you or your sister if they see this?"

I never understood why moms have to worry about daughter's marriage as the first priority and everything else as second, I thought secretly.

Dad tried to stop Mom, but she did not care to listen until she was done. Then she walked away to her room dropping tears like rain. I followed her to the room. I had never seen her in as much pain before. I hugged mom. She hugged me back saying "I hope at least you will never lie to me." Soon, Di burst in tears too. She hugged Dad as tight as she could. She looked scared. "Dad, I am sorry. I promise I will never let you guys down again. I want to confess that I don't want to continue my studies. I have no interest in studies at all."

Dad wanted her to finish her graduation, but couldn't convince her in spite of trying for months after that day. After this incident, Mom and Di never had as friendly a relationship as before for a long time.

After the whole scary, angry, and emotional drama, we all went to bed in our respective rooms. I was sad on what had happened to Di, but a corner in my heart was happy about one thing, that from now on I wouldn't have to hear her stories relating to boys. But that quietness in the room was slaughtering me now. We both lay down on our bed. I held her hand. "Are you OK Di?" I asked, looking at her.

"I don't know," she replied gazing at the slowly moving ceiling fan.

Every night I wished for the quiet time, but that night I didn't like it. That day I realized how much I loved Di and her useless babble. I loved watching her talk, instead of crying. She never understood it though. She never realized how I kept her secrets to myself, in spite of her being wrong most times. She never noticed the small sacrifices I did for her like giving up on my room. But that day for sure this Hitler was calm, maybe more sad than calm. "Soni, can you tell me what they showed on TV about this incident?"

I didn't want her to feel more sad and guilty. So I didn't tell her all the details of what they showed on TV.

After hearing my manipulated version of what they aired on TV, she said, "I made a fool out of myself. I loved him very much and he left me to be alone there when I needed him. I never drink, even if I go to a pub, I only go with him and dance with him. I never knew before this evening that he is into drugs. I insisted a lot to leave as soon as he purchased drugs from one shabby, ugly-looking man. He said 'Wait here one minute, I will hit the restroom and then we will leave.' When he was coming back from the restroom, he sensed something fishy. He understood about the raid looking at scared people and crowd running around like crazy. He also saw one policeman entering another room. So he never came back to the room where he left me alone." She broke into tears again, but kept talking. "I really felt ashamed of my choice— because of which I was there in that situation today— when the news reporter focused the camera on my face saying 'sophisticated-looking people like her are getting into drugs more nowadays. God knows what their parents are doing throwing money at kids to spend like this? Is this our country's future?" Di continued without stopping. "Hearing the news reporter's words, took me into a flashback to realize that I never went to the college to study. I feel ashamed of that. I feel ashamed that I betrayed my parents. Then and there I decided to talk to Mom and Dad about what I want without any more lies."

After a brief pause, she added, "Good Lord, before taking me into the police station, they did some sort of quick test on me and three other girls, who they thought didn't look like were involved in drugs, by taking a saliva swab. In minutes, they confirmed their instincts were right about all the four girls. They released us on the warning to not be seen again at that place or any similar places. When I walked out crying, I saw him waiting in his car. I sat in the car, and asked him to drop me at home. I was scared. I didn't want to get into a taxi alone that late in the night. He kept apologizing, but that didn't matter anymore. When we reached home, while getting out of the car I told him I never want to see him again." Then she wept even louder. I had never seen her like this before. Nobody in our house knew the real story except Di and now me. Mom and Dad didn't bother to hear her side of the story. That was sad and unfair to her, I thought. Mom and Dad always thought Di had been taking drugs that evening.

I hugged her tight and kissed her. She cried out even louder and said, "Please don't tell this to anyone; I *even had sex with him a few times. I feel disgusted now."*

My parents thought Di had changed much after this incident. She changed in certain aspects. But they didn't know the real episode of her life that changed her. Anyways . . . after the real episode, she talked to Mom and Dad about her willingness to get married and settle down. Within a few months, Di got married to a man of our parents' choice.

Chapter 11. Sonia's Predicament

Lost in recollecting the incident of that one Thursday evening, I do not notice Dad standing behind me. I stand still and watch through the window, people walking in and out of our colony. He places his hand on my shoulder breaking my chain of thoughts.

"You are absolutely right. We shouldn't stop you from doing anything just because of mistakes Pahal has made. It is like saying if a child falls while walking, his younger sibling may never walk. That is wrong with all means."

I turn around with a look on my face. "Really? You mean it Dad?" A smile on his face makes me hug him. Then he says, "But something still bothers me." He lets out a long sigh of despair, at least so I thought. Again he continues, "Pahal mentioned about Esha and you."

Seeing the frown on my face, he continues with no delay, "Don't think it's your Di's fault." He then hesitates but says it, "It's just that of late I have heard stories regarding girls or boys . . . you know how in your ragging . . . you and her," he stops saying it. A kind of scorn takes over his calm face. When he can't finish his sentence, a quick shiver goes down my spine.

If Dad feels disgusted to say the word for a girl being in a relationship with another girl, how would he accept the fact of his own daughter getting married to Esha one day? This thought scares the heck out of me and tears roll down my cheek. He wipes my tears and puts that topic to rest for now. "Let's decide about your trip tomorrow after you come home from college. Anyways, you are late to go to bed." But I fail to explain him what is going on right now in my mind. I wish I could talk to him, and share all the secrets buried deep in my heart.

The entire night I toss and turn in my bed, staring at the furniture in the room for no reason. I am petrified with a thought, *one fine morning, how would I share with my family about my relationship with her? What will happen if they come to know from somewhere else?*

All of a sudden, I doubt my sexual orientation, which I never questioned before. *Why all this craziness?* I ask myself without getting any answer. *Why am I different from most of the other girls around me? Is this a phase that will pass away soon? Or is this something that defines me? I want to talk to someone. I want to put my doubts in front of someone. Someone who will help me and guide me to get the answers to all my questions.*

First, I have the urge to call Esha to talk to her about this, but on second thought I want to keep her out of this until I get my own uncertainties cleared up. She is involved in it. I don't want to hurt her feelings sharing my confusion with her. I was the one who started this relationship. I was the one who was sure about it then. I shouldn't share this with her unless I am one hundred percent confident about what is going on in my mind. My head almost bursts with all these questions and hesitations.

There is only one other person I can confide in. But right this minute is an inappropriate time to call. Moreover if Dad is still awake, then his doubts might turn into belief.

In the morning, I pretend to be sick to stay home. Tiredness from lack of sleep somewhat helps to show fatigue on my face.

Luckily, Mom goes out to place the trash bin for the garbage collector. My aunt steps out too at the same time. Mom mentions to her about me not feeling well. Soon Girish stops by to check on me. By that time Dad has left for work and Mom has gone outside our colony to purchase fresh vegetables. That is the perfect time to talk to him.

"What's the matter, girl?" he asks, stepping in when I open the door.

I tell him what happened after he left in the night, just the conversation part between me and Dad.

"Tell me the complete truth. What's going on between you and her?" he asks more assertively than ever before.

"Before I tell you the truth, I have something else that I want to say."

"Say it then," he says casually.

"I am lucky to have a brother—a friend like you that I can confide in. I hope I can count on you for your support," I express.

He lightly smacks the top of my head and says, "You and your sentimental drama . . . don't go well together. Come to the point."

"By the way, when and how did you turn into such a sentimental girl?" he asks followed by a conservative self-chuckle. As usual he tries to lighten my mood. But at the same time, he reads worry in my eyes. The pressure is building up inside me. I can barely hold it in anymore. I need to share it with him, now or never. I take a deep breath, gather all my courage and tell him everything, the truth about her and me. He gets little agitated. "Does that mean you lied when I asked you about your relationship with her? You stated that you girls are only friends."

"Did I have a choice then?" I reply to his question hastily with another question.

He stands up stomping his feet in fury. "I was suspicious about it from the beginning. I think I was a fool to trust you on what you said." His stomp plays out his annoyance. His tone does not match his anger level though.

I weep. Easing his frown, he asks, "If you lied earlier, then why are you sharing this with me now? What do you expect from me?"

"Our families could find out about my relationship with her, at any time. I wanted to share that first with you. There is no one in this house who understands me better than you." I finish my statement and cry out loudly with my hands over my face, covering my eyes.

He comes closer and moves my hands away from my face. Looking into my eyes, he says it in a strong and clear voice, "I understand how you must be feeling, but let me be clear. Regarding this matter, I don't think I can support you going against our family, at least not till I am financially independent. But you should know, off the record, I am always there for you."

He sits next to me. Wrapping his arm around my shoulder, he says in a soft low tone, "By the way, why are you trapping yourself in this situation . . . I mean being with a girl? Have you seriously thought about it?"

He pauses for a second to continue again. "Why don't you try going out with boys, you know what I mean? Once you find the right guy, you may feel differently."

When I give him a strange look, of WTF . . . what are you talking about, taking his hand off my shoulder and backing off a little, he says, "I am just saying."

Then he stands up to go. He is getting late for college. He walks out of my room and turns around. He stands at the entrance of my room door and states, "My dude—Abhay—has been interested in you for a long time. I have been discouraging him. If you want, I can arrange a weekend lunch for you both. He is a nice guy and will be a doctor soon— nice package, huh?" He waits for my response to no avail and walks out saying, "Give it a thought."

Should I try it? Or not? Possibly not. Is this my opportunity to make my own doubts clear about if I am straight, bi, or gay? I am confused. Would it help? Or would it make things even more complicated? The whirlwind of thoughts keep me occupied the whole day. I don't talk to Esha in spite of her five calls since morning. Mom is worried about me. I didn't eat anything the entire day, didn't take Esha's calls, and didn't come out of my room, all of which seemed strange to her.

*****

On her way back home, in the evening, Esha stops by.

"Please, make her eat something," Mom requests, letting her in.

She gives Mom a big bear hug and says, "Don't worry aunty. I got it under control."

That brings a huge smile to Mom's face. This girl's smile, energy level, and attitude, everything is magnetic. I can't be saved.

"You don't look that sick. Why didn't you come?" she demands.

"I had a headache," I reply.

"Liar, liar . . . your PJs are on fire," she chuckles holding the corner of my PJ's left leg. Within a few minutes, she makes me laugh and even eat food.

That is the reason I wanted to stay away from her till I resolve this doubt in my head about what I really want. Her captivating personality can make me do anything for her. I can't even think straight when she is around. But I need to be left alone, especially away from her, to think clearly about my dilemma. If she keeps hovering around me, I can't ruminate about anything else but her. Even though I was the one who took the initiative of this relationship between us, now I am the one who is in doubt. I definitely have to figure out my feelings before moving any further. I owe it to myself to know for sure so I can find peace inside. That's why I myself decide not to go on the college trip. I will get to spend those two days without her and without going to college at all. In short, I will have lots of alone time to ponder over this confusion.

After Esha feeds me the last bite of food, she lands a gentle peck on my cheek, pats my back, "Good job, girl!" Mom is in complete awe of her as usual when she sees the empty plate. A smile dawns on Mom's face that has been missing since morning. She gets back to her work with a sigh of relief.

"Let me guess what happened," Esha says, sitting by my side. She turns to face me and continues, "Uncle didn't sanction you permission for the college trip, right?"

At first, I don't participate in her guessing game. But when she presses too much, I give in to hide the real reason from her. I nod.

"Time for Plan B execution," she adds.

When I give her a prying look asking about details of Plan B, rising on her feet and being very much herself, she says, "You don't worry about it at all. I will handle everything . . . actually my dad will handle everything."

Will uncle talk to my dad about sending me on the school trip? How would Dad react to that? Should I ask her not to get involved in this matter? Should I ask her to let me handle this matter on my own? All these questions, one after another, flood through my mind, but I stay quiet. I am sure I might speak up about my confusion if I talk a lot to her.

*****

A few minutes after Esha leaves, Girish shows up. "Have you decided anything then?" he probes.

"About what?" I pretend not to get the context of his question.

"What about what? Obviously on meeting Abhay. In spite of our exams he is ready, I already talked to him," he finishes his sentence fast to avoid my interruption or perhaps to not give me a chance to say no to it.

I come up with reasons to put it down. "But what if Dad comes to know about it? No, no, I don't want . . . ." Without letting me finish, he jumps in, "This Saturday afternoon, keep yourself available. I will take you with me and believe me, no one would know about this except the three of us."

"Please dress nicely," he says and throws a glance at me before leaving.

How in the world can I handle all this? A voice screams in my head, giving me headache and heartache. Finally, I decide to go with the flow instead of thinking much about it and feeling low.

That night, I eat food before Dad comes home. I don't go out of my room at all after Dad arrives to avoid any further discussion on my college trip. Not because I am scared that he might say no again, but I want to reconsider my willingness to go to the trip, especially when I am stuck in big of a confusion. This trip could be life altering.

After his and Mom's dinner is done, a knock on my room door interrupts an over analysis session that was crowding my thoughts.

"It's open," I say without even looking at who is in the door. I sense that it would be Dad.

"Beta, are you studying?" he asks, entering the room.

Without shifting my gaze from my textbook to him, I respond, "Yes, Dad. Tell me what?" In response to my question, I hope he will ask me what is going on in my mind. What am I so upset about? Is there anything that I would like to share with him?

Reading my mind, he asks me with a small grin, "Why are you upset? I haven't said no to the trip yet."

Tears are all ready to tumble out of my eyes. Fighting back those tears, I instantly wipe them from the corners of my eyes and secretly wish to pop open my heart in front of him, revealing all the secrets that I have stored for years. But I know I can't do it now. Perhaps I might share it with him, but definitely not at this moment, when I am not hundred percent sure myself.

Standing behind my chair, he speaks softly, "I thought a lot about you going on this tour. It was silly of me to consider the ragging incident of you and Esha, in altogether some other way. I trust my Beta and I am sure she won't break my trust."

Hearing those words from him, I can't fight back my tears any longer. I cry it out. Now, I am even more worried, since he shows great trust in me. My apprehensions are double fold now. How would I face him if ever I share my secret with him? When I don't stop crying after a few moments, he adds, placing his hand on my head, "Now that you are going on the trip, you should jump with joy and not weep like this." That puts a temporary smile on my face. Crying out loud helps a lot, I believe.

Before leaving the room, he wishes me good night and mentions, "By the way . . . Esha's dad called me to talk about your college tour. She told him I am not allowing you to go. Even before his call, I had decided. I told him you are going."

If it wouldn't have been about my predicament that currently blocks everything else from entering my mind, for sure, I would have been jumping up and down like a small kid to go on the trip.

Chapter 12. An odd date

Saturday

GIRISH CALLS AT AROUND 9:30 in the morning. He reminds me, "We have to leave at 11:00 sharp. I guess one and a half hours should be good enough for you to groom yourself."

My brother firmly believes my relationship with her will not do me any good, at least his actions say so. Otherwise, he had never been my reminder about any of the plans. Many times, in fact, he forgot about them and then got ready in just minutes.

"OK, I will be ready," I say and hang up the phone.

These last few days, I have been thinking way too much on whether I should go out with Abhay or not. While eating, while on the train, and even while taking a bath each day, I have been thinking about this. After this morning's reminder call from Girish, I go to the bathroom to freshen up. In the gentle shower, when each droplet of cold water touches my body, it feels as if each water drop hits me stronger than the earlier drip, screaming at me, "You crazy girl, you love her earnestly. Why are you fooling yourself and that poor guy Abhay?"

Today, the shower no longer feels refreshing. After washing and coming back to my room, I sit on my bed with a blank mind as if I have lost the ability to think. An inner voice inside me tries to contemplate loud enough that I cannot hear myself. I can't think clearly. There is no question that I love to spend time with her, be around her. But right now, I am curious to understand myself. I want things crystal clear in my head first. I want to settle the bewilderment that is born inside my head of late. I want to be 100% sure whether I am gay. In all honesty, I should have thought about it before getting closer to her. But it never appeared as confusing then.

Setting aside my doubts, I wear a cheerful smile and get ready to soak up this experience. I try hard to concentrate all my focus on Abhay. It's been a little over two years since I had last seen him. When in school, I was always part of Girish and his group. Abhay was part of our gang too. A charming personality, 5' 9" tall, slim, with a dimple on the right side of his cheek, always smiling and spreading that smile to people around him. In many ways, he is like Esha. He too has a great dressing style, one more thing in common with her.

On Girish's suggestion, I go for a feminine look today. I choose a pastel pink chiffon short kurti, which has, sparsely distributed, decorative patterns adorned with stones and crystals, paired with matching ¾ length leggings, which ends just above my ankle. I bought this kurti-legging a year ago but have never worn it until now. I accessorize it with a silver base bracelet that has pastel pink flowers and pink transparent and shiny crystal beads. My Jiju bought it for me once when Di and he went to a jewelry exhibition somewhere in New Mumbai. When I see myself in the mirror, after getting ready, I can't believe what I see. That kurti fits perfect on me, showing curves in the right places.

"Wow! Never knew I could look this captivating," I boast under my breath, looking in the mirror, turning from one side to the other, like I have never done before.

Suddenly, I hear a knock on my room door. "Let's go, we don't want to be late," Girish directs.

"Coming . . ." I say, applying nude lip-gloss.

"OK, let's go," I continue and open my room door.

I see looks of astonishment on his and Mom's faces staring at me. "Soni, you look pretty. You should stop wearing those jeans. You should only wear these kinds of dresses," she says, hugging me, followed by a question, "Where are you both going?"

I flat-out gaze at him as if I ask him to reply to Mom's question. Then I turn my focus to putting on silver high-heel sandals with an adjustable ankle strap. Those belonged to Di in the past. After she got married, her accessories that she didn't want, I inherited. I almost never wore those. They come in handy today.

He gives a prompt reply to Mom's question. "Aunty, I am bored with studying. I need to watch a movie. And anyways, we have watched no movie together for a long time. We will have our lunch out too." We get out of there fast enough to be in the elevator to avoid any further questions from Mom.

"Wow . . . Soni. Can't believe you look stunning," he praises, gazing at me.

"Thank you, thank you," I reply with my heart full of joy. All of a sudden, I feel special because of the compliments I get, first from Mom then him.

"Let me tell you . . . today, Abhay will go crazy for sure," he says, winking at me.

On impulse, I hit him hard and come out of the gooey haze of all these compliments to reality. Hearing Abhay's name, I again realize of what will happen next, which I somewhat forgot, while being engrossed in getting ready. Today I liked getting dressed up in a way as I never enjoyed.

I think in my mind, *If Esha could see me at this moment, she would for sure love my new look. A rather rare look.*

From nowhere, I again get nervous about going on a date with Abhay. I have known him for years and have cherished many memories with him, being part of the same hangout gang. I worry whether this meeting with him will help me to clear out my perplexity. Then how would I ever mention it to him? My palms become sweaty. A weird fear settles inside me. As soon as we step out of the elevator, Abhay comes out of his BMW 3 sports car. He parked it under a tree shadow, right across from our building. He hails from a rich family. Both his parents are well-known surgeons in Mumbai. His dad gifted him this car when he got into medical school. He hugs Girish tight and says, "Thanks buddy." They are pals since childhood. They share an awesome rapport. Words like thanks and sorry don't exist between them. But still Abhay thanked him today for setting this date. Then he turns to me, hugs me to greet as always. But the way he embraces me today feels different. Typically, Abhay and I both share a carefree and oh-my-buddy kind of attitude toward each other while interacting. But today it has a hint of care, tenderness and nervousness.

"You look splendid in this outfit," he says with a charming smile, his eyes gleaming.

I reply with a plain thank you, forcing a grin on my face.

Abhay holds the car door for me, to let me in the car. Girish sits in the navigator's seat while I sit in the back seat, right behind Abhay. I sense his state of happiness from his ear to ear grin and glint in his eyes. He talks to Girish, but every so often he looks at me in the rear view mirror.

*****

After we drop Girish in a cafe, I move to the navigator's seat. We both are awfully quiet. I am hushed because I am still pondering over how he would react if he knew my reason to be here with him today. Should I tell him everything about the confusion I am going through or not? He doesn't speak a word because he is too excited and nervous to talk. I can read his expressions.

He turns on the music. A song that I have never heard plays.

Baby, baby, can't you hear my heartbeat?

As song starts, he stares at me; I notice it from corner of my eye. As soon as I gaze at him, he looks away with a gentle smile. I am stirred by the song; it tells everything that he wants to say. Now, I don't know how to be oblivious to his expressions any more, like I have been pretending all this time since he picked us up.

"What's bothering you, Soni?" he asks, breaking his own quietness.

"Me? Nothing," I reply hastily.

"You are not your usual self . . .umm. . . easygoing and naughty like I have always seen you."

I shrug my shoulders, twitching my lower lip. I scold myself inside my head. *Soni, you are here to spend time with him, on kind of date with him. You wanted to have this experience to resolve your dilemma. Now stop acting like a pig head. Talk to him . . . in a courteous manner.*

He recalls, out loud so it's audible, many memorable, funny moments that we, as members of a group, shared. I also narrate a couple of unforgettable incidents. Remembering those days, our jaws hurt from continuous laughter and wide grins. To my surprise, I enjoy his company all over again, as I always have. Even before I realize, we reach an exclusive restaurant in west Mumbai. It is dark inside the restaurant, as if nighttime, with dim lights on. Each table has one daisy flower in a thin spiral shape flask, paired with a candle. The ceiling of the restaurant is decorated as the sky with a full moon and many stars. It is peaceful and romantic. The hostess whisks us to our table, in a corner, discreet and elegant. I am in complete awe of his choice.

The candlelight, illuminating his dimple, makes him appear even more amiable. I always complimented him the most in our whole gang, for his choice and style of clothes, the way he carried himself, and everything about him. But today, I don't compliment him even once. Should I or should I not? I again think way too much. I suppose that happens to everyone, when one is stressed, confused, and indecisive.

It doesn't take long for that place to play its magic. He glances at me, with a smile touching his face. Then, in a deep, concerned voice, he says "Soni, when you smile, you look your best. Always keep smiling."

We order food. Our conversation continues again from where we left in the car. It is amazing going through the same jokes, recollecting the mischievous and all the good and bad times that we had spent together, as if we are knitting a fabric of old memories, lying spread on the table, right between us. The more time I spend with him today, the more I realize that I don't see my strings getting attached to him, in any other way than through the fabric of old memories. But I tenaciously read his eyes. His bright eyes are saying more, longing for more and revealing more than his words. Even though, we have fun recollecting the old times, deep inside I miss Esha's presence. I miss her being at my side in this romantic place.

From nowhere, he breaks the flow of our conversation. Setting aside old memories, he compliments me once more, "This outfit suits you. You look gorgeous and sexy."

I am speechless, not knowing what to say. Part of me feels wonderful, thinking, *There is someone in this world who loves me like crazy—not only is he expressing it in words, but also I am seeing it in his eyes, sitting right in front of him.* The other part is not sure what to do and is confused.

I thank him and return the compliment, "You look dashing as always, my handsome (that is how I always addressed him before)." That puts a twinkle in his eyes like a small kid, who gets a candy that he dearly wanted. It is certain that he has missed me addressing him that way.

He looks in my eyes, touches my bracelet with his fingers. "These beautiful flowers of the bracelet, they look exquisite because you are wearing them." Slowly, he moves his fingers from the bracelet toward my palm and confesses, "You don't know how long I waited for this day to come—to take you on a date. I can't express in words how much I have longed for you." He pauses and holds my palm gently. Immediately, I take my hand away from his, moving my gaze from him to the flower on the table. I stir in my position to hide my awkwardness.

He continues, in a softer tone than before, "But I also respect your choice. I don't know what Girish mentioned to you or why you agreed to come out. But I certainly see you are nervous. There is something that is bothering you whenever I try to express my feelings for you."

Not knowing how to respond, I stay quiet because he is right. I am nervous and preoccupied with Esha's thoughts. After a few minutes of sheepish silence between us, we make a move from there.

Before returning to the cafe where we dropped Girish, I break the silence. He looks hurt from my behavior. I feel guilty that I shouldn't have come out with him knowing my situation. "Abhay, I truly had a good time recollecting old memories with you. I am sorry if I hurt you at all; trust me, it was not intended."

"No worries, take your time. If you want to share anything, you know—*banda hazeer hain*—I am here for you."

While in the elevator, going back to our home, Girish inquires about the time I spent with Abhay. He asks, "How was it?" The elevator is filled with quietness since I am not sure yet how to respond to his question. Nudging me, he asks, "Isn't he crazy for you, as I mentioned?"

How could I deny that fact? But again I have my own reasons to not to accept it aloud. "I am not sure how it went," I reply in a soft low voice. Contradictory to my answer, I know deep inside my heart that I have found the answers to my questions. My dilemma is resolved. I just pray that voice inside me takes me in the right direction. Because, once decided, I can't ever go back.

CHAPTER 13. I LOVE HER

"HOW WAS THE MOVIE?" Mom asks opening the door to let me in.

Even before I can open my big mouth to speak the lie relating to the movie I never watched, she says, "Esha called twice asking for you. Call her. It seems she wanted to talk you urgently about an assignment."

"OK, I will." Saying this, I walk right into my room closing the door behind me. I don't call her immediately. I want to have a long chat with her, which I haven't done in the last few weeks. Today, I wish to spend time with her. It didn't take a long time to clear out the dilemma from my head—just a few hours of my, Abhay, and Girish's time—but it feels long enough to make me mentally exhausted. These last two weeks, I have been ignoring her. But, the more I was avoiding her, the more I was yearning for her.

"But, now I am transparent on what I want—no matter what I have to go through to be with her, I will," I assure myself.

But before I see her or converse with her, I need a little more time to settle down—to settle the dust off my mind of the whole dilemma episode. I don't want to share that saga with her; unnecessarily, she might get hurt.

"OK, then I will call her tomorrow." Saying it out loud, I sit down on my bedside. I want to listen to music to get energized. I turn on the music system that Dad gifted me—actually I asked for it—when I was accepted into engineering, a few months back.

*****

When I am completely engrossed in the music, Mom howls while knocking on the door of my room, "Soni, pick up the phone. It's Esha."

I didn't even hear the phone ringing. Mom picked it up from the other line and then informed me. The music is working its magic, I think. I feel relaxed and happy.

"Hi Esha . . . ," I say, turning down the music volume.

"Soni, expect me at your house shortly. I need to talk to you. You have been behaving weird, neglecting me. I need to know right now what's up with you," she finishes off blazing fast. Without giving me a chance to utter a single word, she hangs up. As soon as I put the handset down, the phone rings again.

"OMG, are you OK, Di?" I raise my voice. Mom rushes to my room to know more of what's happening on the other end of the phone.

"Don't worry Di. Stay put. Mom and Dad will be there in a few minutes," I say hearing Di's voice, which sounds as if she is in more shock than in pain. After explaining everything to Mom, I call Dad and Girish.

Di is in the third month of her pregnancy. She slipped in the bathroom. Her ankle as well as belly is hurting her a lot. I hope, Di doesn't have a fractured ankle, and the baby is fine too. Mom and Dad will go to the doctor with her. They both will go to Di's house first, Mom from here and Dad coming from his shop. Girish accompanies Mom; since he is studying medicine, our family wants him by their side for all medical-related decisions.

When Mom is leaving, Esha reaches our home. Mom asks her to stay the night at our house, thinking she and Dad might have to stay with Di. Jiju is out of town for his business work. Esha is delighted to stay with me and so am I. Without wasting any time, she calls her mom and permission is granted, as if she has a magic wand that works perfectly fine as usual. I brief her on Di's condition and we both pray for her good health.

Immediately following this turmoil, Esha blasts question after question. I don't want to answer any of her questions; better yet, I wish to avoid them. To divert her mind, I take her to my room. Di's news stirred me and Mom. None of us noticed the music in my room was playing all this time. The pleasant music beats fall on her ears leaving her forgetful about her questions. Thank God for that. We both jig with the beats of the song, gentle, slow, flirtatious, and caressing. It is a Zen-like feeling being with her, dancing with her, forgetting about all the worries of the world. The song— Love is All Around— starts and is perfect for the moment.

We dance a bit more. Suddenly, I stop dancing. With the music still running in the background, I get closer to her. My heart is pounding too hard. It is intense but sweet. Tucking a stroke of her hair behind her ear, I look into her eyes, which seem even more beautiful than ever before. Caressing my hand from her lips to her nape, I pull her toward me. She steps back a little. I can see nervousness and craving, all at the same time, in her vivacious eyes. This otherwise bold girl is always uneasy when it comes to taking our relationship to the next level.

With a gentle smile, tenderly I say, "I don't think it's wrong … I love you."

I go near her again. I hold Esha's hand and kiss it with affection. She stands still with her eyes closed and a smile touching her lips. Slowly and gently, I slip off her loosely fitted tunic from her right shoulder, tracing my lips from her neck down to her shoulder. Gradually, she relaxes and bites fondly on my ear, which leaves me shaking in delight. Softly, I slither my hands inside her tunic. As my hands caress her breasts, she breathes heavily, bringing her lips closer to mine. She tugs at my dress and strokes my breasts, leaving me gasping. It seems an adrenaline rush has swept away her nervousness. She leads me to the bed, pushing me to lie down. Then she kisses every inch of me. She wants me as bad as I want her. We both have more appetite for each other than I imagined. I am seeing an altogether different side of her that I love to the core.

Esha is gliding down exploring each part of my body, taking charge of loving me as never before. There is no stopping her now. The trace that she is making with her lips on my waist gives me permanent marks of pleasure. She is panting as she goes further down. A gusty wave bursts inside me leaving me shattered in a million glorious pieces. I can't stop saying, "Love you Esha, I love you."

She finally slows down and lies beside me. Her fingers are still tracing my naked body. She is still breathless, but saying, "Love you, Soni."

All of a sudden, we hear heavy pounding on our home's main door. This scares the hell out of us.

When we hear the banging on the door again, Esha starts crying. I don't have time to console her. I put on my dress. Then I pick up her tunic and jeans from the floor and toss them to her. Quickly I run to the door after getting dressed and fixing my hair in place. She follows me in a few moments. Girish's mom has been ringing the doorbell for a long time. She thought I was all by myself at home, so she wanted to check on me. Since I didn't respond to the doorbell, she got worried and pounded the wooden door too hard. I had to explain to her. The music was playing and we were dancing, as a result couldn't quite hear the bell buzzing. After she leaves, we sigh in relief, followed by hugs and giggles.

"Hey, you are gorgeous," I say kissing her again gently over her shoulder and clasping her tighter as if not to let her go, never ever. Nuzzling my cheek, she is about to say something, when our home phone rings. We rush to pick it up.

It's Mom. She mentions that they are leaving the doctor's office to come home. Esha and I quickly go to a small temple built on an altar in a corner of the living room. We bow down in front of God, say our small prayers. This is our way to thank Him for Di and baby's well-being. Di got a sprain in her ankle, but luckily no fracture. They will bring her home instead of staying at her house. That means, sadly enough, Esha has to leave once they arrive. I wanted her to stay.

I figure Di must be starving. Esha and I cook for her. It is as much fun working side by side in the kitchen with my girl as it is to paint with her. We spend more time together in the evening before Dad and I drop her off at her house.

*****

Di is glowing in spite of being in severe pain. After spending a few days with us, she leaves when Jiju comes back from his business trip. She feels much better now. All these days, Mom made lip-smacking food for the yummy to be mommy. I am not sure about Di but I definitely loved it all. As Di and Jiju enter the elevator to leave, our phone rings.

I rush and speak, "Hello," picking up the phone.

"Hi, Soni. This is Abhay," he says.

"Hey hi," I reply in a low voice, thinking it is good that Di has left otherwise she would have grilled me, which, as always, is annoying. Her enquiries would have started even before me hanging up the phone. Who's calling, why he is calling you, what's going on and what not?

"So?" he asks followed by a silence; maybe he wants to talk further on what I didn't let him say when we went out on a date.

"So . . . what's up?" I fill in the gap.

"Would you like to go out with me again?" comes a deep male voice from the other side of the phone's ear piece.

"Oh sure," I want to say, not because I am dying to hear what he couldn't finish saying that day, but because I want to share something with him, something that I feel special about. When I don't reply quickly, he entreats, "Please."

"If you say please that sweetly, how can I say no," I respond, laughing.

"OK, then. I will pick you up on Saturday afternoon," he announces in delight. Then he continues, "Can't believe I am damn lucky, two Saturdays in a row with you." His voice tells me how overjoyed he is at the moment.

Interrupting that joy, I respond, "But, on one condition."

"Anything for you, dear," he gives in without knowing my condition. Wow, he loves me too much is my first thought. But my condition is very simple. I don't want Girish to join us this time. I want to go out with him alone. Then I want to tell him about the special person of my life; Girish wouldn't let me do that. I can't, anymore, fool him around. He has every right to know about my zero interest in the relationship with him.

*****

I get more and more nervous as Saturday comes closer. I don't know how in the world I will explain this to him. Secretly, at one moment, I hope he understands it all the way and promises to be my friend for life, to be at my side whenever I need him. At another moment, I feel selfish, just thinking about myself, my relationship with Esha and me needing help from him. What about his feelings? I certainly do care for his feelings, but I can't help it. My heart and my emotional state are beyond the control of my mind. All I know is I can't keep it as a secret anymore from such an awesome guy like Abhay. He deserves the best in life.

I practice it all—what I will say, how I will say it—like . . . not 1, 2, 3 . . . but I practice it many more times; after fifteen I lose the count. Still, I am panicky.

*****

"Heck, with your nervousness. Just tell him!" I scold myself before leaving to meet Abhay. Unlike last Saturday, I spend no time thinking about what to wear and what not to. I opt for boot-cut white jeans pants with an orange color top, fresh looking. I take a few deep breaths while waiting for him outside our colony gate. That helps me relax. As soon as I sit in the car, he turns to pick up a flower bouquet from the car's back seat. He looks dashing as always; it's hard not to notice that. Handing those nice orchid flowers to me, he lands a peck on my cheek, leaving me surprised.

He brought nothing last Saturday, on our first date, then why today? I think in my mind. Maybe that day Girish was with us and he wanted to avoid all this.

"Thank you for the beautiful flowers," I say, looking at the flowers and avoiding his gaze. *Oh boy! Flowers and this peck . . . need to tell him sooner before he surprises me with something else.*

I am nervous again to share with him what I planned to. My breathing gets a little heavier because of uneasiness, a chaos of thoughts going through my mind. I look outside the window of the car to ease myself. I look at the crowd outside on the road. Everybody is running, trying to reach their destinations, some are going home, some to school, colleges, and some to work. Everybody is trying to achieve their goal. And here I am sitting without even trying to achieve my today's objective. I aim to share the special secret with him.

He turns on music. A song 'And I love her' by The Beatles (he mentions that song is by the Beatles) plays. I can resonate with every line of that song. It makes my job easier. The practice that I have done for the last few days, on how to say, what to say to him about Esha, doesn't help. But this song does.

In a calm, low voice, I express, "Abhay, I love her." The song is still playing in the background. And I assert myself in my heart that a love like hers and mine could never die.

"What did you say?" he demands.

"I love her . . ." followed by a small pause. I reaffirm, more firmly this time, "Abhay, I love Esha."

His first reaction—slamming the car breaks—-ends; luckily we are safe. Then he parks outside an Archies Gallery that we were about to pass. He rests his head on the steering wheel. All of a sudden, an awkward silence is dominant between us, shutting out the surrounding noise and crowd. I don't know what to say any more. Rather, I want him to ask me something, anything about me and her. After a few minutes of quietness, he looks up, turns a little, to stare at me. I see water flowing in his eyes. He tries hard to not let out. I look down at my hands, the knuckles of one hand pressing against the palm of the other. I feel shamefaced for calling him out for a date last week, to break his heart, in a brutal way like this, only in one week. But he leaves me amazed one more time.

"Don't worry about me, Soni. I will be fine," he says with a weary voice, swallowing his tears.

Patting my head, what he says leaves me startled. "You don't have to tell me anything if you don't feel comfortable. But let me tell you, I respect your decision, whatever it may be. And I always will."

I break into tears. How could I not tell him? He is such a dear friend and moreover an awesome person. I ask him, "Can we go to some place where we can sit and talk? I want to share with you whatever is in my mind, how I feel and everything." He takes me to a café where nobody knows us.

He first cries, "I am sad that you can't be mine." But then he immediately expresses with a wide forceful smirk, in a typical formal way, "Please consider this as my golden promissory note. I am your friend forever. I will always support and respect your decision." That brings an ear to ear smile on my face. I can't thank him enough. Our so-called date (it's ironic, I still call the time I spent with him as a date), ends agreeably.

*****

When I narrate the whole story to Girish about my and Abhay's meeting, he gets mad at me. He fumes in anger. I am not quite sure why he is furious—after all he has known this for a while. Possibly because I told everything to his best friend, and he is scared that he might lose a friend for he forced me to go out with him. Or maybe, he doesn't like the fact that I am gay. I guess nobody in my family would like it.

Girish's anger doesn't last for too long. He settles in a few days, but his stand is still the same. He won't support me in this, going against the family. Secretly, in my heart, I don't know why but I knew he would.

CHAPTER 14. OUR SECRET IS OUT

December 2003
Mahabaleshwar, India

COUNTDOWN BEGINS, two more days to go. I have been marking the calendar for the last few days. I can't wait any more to go on our college trip. Our entire class is excited. The thought of spending three days and two nights in Esha's company is electrifying. Even though we both know we won't be able to give whole lots of attention to each other being surrounded by other classmates and teachers, but still, we can at least walk hand in hand, and can enjoy each other's presence twenty-four seven. We, together, shopped for this getaway, and have bought many matching things like accessories, handbags, even pairs of shoes. It's fun.

We leave early Friday morning at around 6:30 to reach Mahabaleshwar at noon, with one stop for breakfast. We enjoy freshly made vada pav—

affectionately called Indian burger or common man's food. Many people in Mumbai eat it every day for breakfast or for lunch. It is not only cheap but also delicious. We enjoy vada pav with cutting tea. Before breakfast, most of us were a little lazy and sleepy. But after a cup of tea, the fun begins. On the bus, we play a nonstop game of Antakshri—a spoken parlor game played in India, freestyle group dancing on Bollywood songs, screaming, hooting, and teasing each other. Never ending fun! We don't realize when we reach Mahabaleshwar Temple.

Our seniors had already shared the little secret about the first spot we would go to. One of our professors, being superstitious, did things certain ways, always in the exact same order. So here we are at Mahabaleshwar Temple, dedicated to Lord Shiva and one of the important pilgrimage sites for Hindus. Mahabaleshwar, a hill resort of India, procures its grand name from 'Mahabali', meaning, 'the one with great power'. The mighty God of destruction, Lord Shiva, is worshipped as Mahabali here. The temple is six kilometers north of the main city. Surrounded by a five-foot-high stone wall, this temple secures Lord Shiva's trishul, Rudraksha, damru, and a bed, which are around 300 years old. The temple also has a raised platform which is square-shaped. According to folklore, the Maratha ruler, Shivaji Maharaj, weighed his mother Jijabai in gold at this platform and then gave away the gold in charity.

The next place that we visit is Panchganga Temple, located next to Mahabaleshwar Temple. Water from five different rivers—Koyna, Krishna, Venna, Savitri, and Gayatri—meet in this place. The convergence of five rivers has given this place the name Panchganga where Panch means five and Ganga means river. All five rivers emerge out of a cow's mouth, which is carved out of stone in this temple. This temple has two jalkunda (jal meaning water and kund meaning tank), named Brahma kund, which is used for bathing and drinking water, and Vishnu kund, which is used for washing clothes and utensils. Should I have known then that Brahma kunda would be the reason that Esha would get hurt, I would never have allowed her to go there. But maybe it was destined to happen. When many of us stride down the stairs of Brahma kunda, she is one of us. She insists I join her. I don't want to go. After getting down two stairs, she turns around to look up at me. She gestures to plead with me to come with her and tries to get down one more step at the same time. Her gaze is on me, instead of on the stairs. Even before anyone can realize what is happening, she lands herself with a sprained ankle. Standing a few feet away from her, I scream when she falls, and she bursts into tears, caused by pain. Immediately the teachers give her the anti-inflammatory ointment and pain killers.

In an hour, Esha walks again, screaming and having fun, but she is limping. I hold her hand and walk with her to make sure she does not pressure her injured ankle. Under my breath, I pray that it doesn't get worse by constant moving around. We both want to make this trip memorable for us, but certainly not in this way.

Soon we are out of the temple, and everybody is hungry. Bus takes us to Venna Lake, one of the most popular tourist attractions here at Mahabaleshwar. Several small eateries line the banks of the lake. After filling our tummies with food, we take a nice walk to the city market. The sun is soft and solacing. The walk is pleasant for all of us, except for Esha. This walk puts much pressure on her freshly injured, young, but weak at the moment, ankle. She moves around with a forced smile on her face. We have a fun time boating on the lake where she doesn't have to move her leg.

When most of us relish the experience of horse riding, she and I, instead sit and relax in nature's bounty for a while. She rests her head on my shoulder.

Next we know that we are going to Bombay Point, also known as Sunset point, the vantage spot—to see the varied shades of the setting sun. On the left side of Bombay Point, lies the lover's point of Mahabaleshwar. As lovers, we are enthusiastic about it. The romanticism of visiting such a spot, when our love is still springing up, is amazing. The way her ankle pain is increasing, I am doubtful that we will make it to that point. But my brave girl takes more pain killers and applies anti-inflammatory ointment again. I am glad that she did it; we truly enjoyed the experience.

The sweet nothings that we exchange say it all that we have been strongly feeling for each other. Especially to have Esha express it, since she has never been the one to take that initiative, makes me fly to heaven, oblivious to the world around me. Little did I know then that this precious feeling of flying to heaven would turn into the sadness and loneliness of hell soon.

One of our classmates, Shikha—the same girl who is Di's neighbor—catches us exchanging special glances at lover's point. As soon as we notice that, suddenly, we both—Esha and I—giggle so as to distract Shikha from her thoughts that sprout in her wicked head.

Once we reach our hotel, every one of us is tired, but still we continue to blabber and chat more. Thinking economically, our professors arrange one room for three girls and likewise for boys too. Shikha wants to join us in our room as the third room partner. Because of her blunt and gossipy nature, many of our classmates dislike her. Esha doesn't have any problems with her, but little does she know Shikha has already been bitching about us to my Di. Apart from this one problem, I have no other complaints with Shikha. Esha crashes as soon as we enter the room. She cries from severe pain as the night's low temperature causes more stiffness in her ankle. It looks more swollen than it looked a few hours back. Now, she needs support to even walk from the bed to the bathroom which is attached to the room and located no more than five feet from the bed. The poor girl suffers and cries the entire night. Shikha and I too toss and turn, thump and bump throughout the night. I am glad that Esha finally sleeps, even though for only a bit.

Early in the morning, we receive the wakeup call that our professors arranged for each one of our rooms. Shikha comes down with a slight fever, maybe because of the change in climate as compared to Mumbai, then exertion from the whole day with the addition of no sleep in the night. Esha suffers from ankle pain, so much that I think it's not worth going to Pratapgarh Fort, the next spot to visit, of our three-day trip. Our professors agree. I decide to stay with her in case if she needs any help. I suggest Shikha to stay with us too. She needs to rest as well. But she swallows one paracetamol and is ready to go.

*****

After the gang leaves for Pratapgarh Fort, the entire morning, Esha and I talk about when and how we want to share our love epic with our parents. Deep down in our hearts, we both know that it will be difficult for both of our parents to handle this. We come up with friendly ideas, nice gestures to share it with them. Esha suggests, "How about we make gajar halwa—carrot confection—for our parents at our respective homes. Once cooked, pour it in a nice container, and then using dry fruits, we should write on it, 'I am gay.' Then leave it at the dining table and go away from there for a while." I like her idea. But for at least one more year, I want to keep it under cover. On the other hand, she believes, the sooner we tell them, the better it is. I don't know about her parents, but for sure, this is not the right time to share it with my family, especially when Dad has recently showed his concern, just hearing it from Di. God knows what would happen if I share with him now.

After a few hours of chit-chat, putting our endless talk on pause, she takes a shower. Helping her to get into the bath tub, I come out of the bathroom, thinking to catch a few minutes of relaxing, me time. I am exhausted from lack of sleep and yesterday's whole day of roaming around. In a bit, after I step out of the bathroom, Esha bellows aloud. I run to the bathroom to make sure she is fine.

"Thank God, I only shut the bathroom door and didn't lock it," I say out loud while running toward it. A soap bar slipped from her hand and fell right on her foot of the hurt ankle.

Luckily she didn't get hurt as bad. She is fine. Otherwise God knows how in the world I would have carried her out of the tub all by myself. Her taller body frame compared to mine would have made the job difficult for me, I think with a sigh of relief. Immediately following, another thought pops into my naughty head. *If I could, I wouldn't mind carrying her, especially the way I see her at this moment,* which leaves me with a mischievous smile, making my thought transparent to her. From nowhere, her gestures change. She looks even more gorgeous with her damp hair and wet body. In spite of being in much ankle pain, the spunk with which she responds to my playful smile oozes with her desire too. Giving in to our passions, I join her for a shower. I stroke her cheeks. She comes closer, melting our damp and warm naked bodies. She starts to move her lips on me. She moves from my lips to my nape with her one hand stroking my thighs. "Love - you - so - much," she pants throughout. We both are lost in our own worlds that we wish should never end. The state of ecstasy we are in, suddenly turns into an uproar of fear and embarrassment when we see Shikha and Mrs. Navandar inside the bathroom. Shikha screams and yells, "I knew it! I knew it. Nobody believed me, but I knew it."

"Oh . . . shit," I exclaim. I curse myself for not locking the bathroom door when I got in with her. Esha is about to faint. Her eyes swim in tears. Mrs. Navandar hurriedly grabs two towels hanging on a hook on the wall and throws them at us.

Hearing Shikha's screech, somebody pounds on the room door. Mrs. Navandar tries to stop her from opening the door to no avail. But she opens the door, as if some show is going on, letting in Professor Mrs. Pande. Oh well, for her it's nothing less than a show. She got the concrete material for her gossip mill. Then there is no stopping Shikha and Madam Pande to spread it all over the world.

Shikha's fever went up, and she felt dizzy as soon as they reached Pratapgarh Fort. Mrs. Navandar and Mrs. Pande accompanied Shikha to drop her off with us. Each of the room partners got one key to the room. I wished, I should have thought about it before.

That's it. Our trip ends then and there. Not only the trip, my and Esha's lovely world is finished. The beautiful life that we both dreamt off together, vanishes right there.

The secret is out!

CHAPTER 15. LOVE DOESN'T ASK WHY

MADAM PANDE makes a few phone calls right in front of us. Her side of the conversation, which we can hear, tears us apart. The ferocity, with which she talks about the whole incident and the look that she gives us, breaks me down. I too start crying. How could she describe us as two sick girls and declare we are taboo for our college? She is told by our Principal, to send both of us back to the college with Mrs. Navandar. Even before we leave, the whole troop is called back in the hotel. The news spreads like fire. Most of our classmates give us a look as if we have committed a severe crime. After some tears, I brace myself. I console myself, *It's OK. People will disapprove of it initially, but if this is what I want, so be it. I have to stand strong.*

Inside I am completely terrified by the thought of facing my mom, dad, and the entire family, even though I stand strong before leaving for Mumbai. The pain of all that is going on around us is much more than Esha's ankle pain. She doesn't take my support, any more, while walking; instead she takes every step with a limp leg and eyes full of tears. I secretly pray for her recovery and ask for strength to face the battle that has to come. On our way back, Mrs. Navandar hugs both of us, saying, "I can only imagine how hard it must be for you girls. But if this is what you want, stay strong. Nothing—that is against the norms of society—can be achieved easily. Breaking norms takes courage and sacrifice. Keep the passion and love for each other alive, but don't let that tolerance trail behind. Remember, this is only the start of the journey; the road ahead is bumpy. Make your choices carefully and thoughtfully." It feels as if God answered my prayers to give both of us strength through her kind and enriching words. I affirm to myself one more time, *No matter what people say, no matter how difficult and painful the journey will be, I am who I am. I will face this truth today with all my inner strength. No more giving in.*

We are taken directly to the college. Our parents are there as well. It looks like before we reach Mumbai, the board members of the college, along with the Principal had a meeting to discuss the situation. They announce, "This act sets bad examples for the other students. We don't want to support this. By expelling Sonia we will let other students know, this and any similar act is not accepted at any cost." Wait a minute . . . why Sonia only? I don't understand at first. But slowly, everything unravels in my head, when I overhear our Principal explaining to Mrs. Navandar, when she questions the decision, asking why not both, why just Sonia? According to the board members, our relationship could affect the reputation of the college, which might harm the fundraising for the college education fund. By expelling me, the partnership between us two girls will be broken. And that will spare the college from getting into the news for wrong, unethical reasons— something that our society doesn't support. Hence no fundraising issues will arise.

But the real reason is something else. It is kept under cover. Esha's dad has been one of the board members of the college for many years now. He donates a big chunk of money to the college fundraising every year, thus she gets the benefit. How, I don't know, but I can read her mind. She is not happy with the decision either. The board's decision causes more grief and frustration to both of us.

This whole episode leaves my parents devastated. I couldn't understand which thing left them more shattered, whether me being gay or me being expelled from college. I guess I know, but I want to stay in denial.

When we reach home, I can't hold back my tears anymore. Dad doesn't utter a single word for a few hours. He doesn't even let Mom talk to me either. This is the worst type of grief and punishment my parents can give me, the Silence. My face is swollen and eyes puffy from crying for a few hours. I want Dad to say something, anything about it. I want him to talk to me.

Di comes to know from Shikha's parents, in fact their whole neighborhood knows by now. How could Di not show up then to add more kerosene on the already burning fire? She enters the house with a chip on her shoulder and says, "See Dad, I cautioned you many times, but you didn't listen." When Dad doesn't respond, she comes to my room yelling, as if to accuse me, "Soni, I knew something is wrong. I warned you before and you just shut me off saying there is nothing like that, we are just friends. This news is spreading like fire in our neighborhood and now on my in-laws' side too."

Dad follows her to my room. Nobody takes part in her conversation. Finally, she shakes me hard, holding my upper left arm, "Do you even realize what - a - shame - you - are - on - our - family? Our neighbors are calling me and asking me about you and her in shameful, weird ways. And, wait till the news spreads in this colony, it will be even more horrendous. This is not the way to explore your curiosity. Do you get me?" she demands.

When I don't say a word, she lets go of my arm, which has already hurt by now because of her tight grip. All this physical pain goes unnoticed compared to the heartache of my family not supporting me. I wish things would not have come out the way they have. She is the same Di whom I have always supported, but she never has realized that.

Dad's muteness has been killing me for so long. He at last breaks the hush.

"Pahal, leave Soni alone for now. We will talk tomorrow."

She shouts in Dad's face, "You are still not saying a word to her, why Dad?" Then she turns around and smacks hard on my head and says, clenching her teeth, "What you are doing is way off beam. At least try to explore some boys, you crazy, sick girl." Then she leaves the room.

That ticks me off and I run behind her to the living room. "Di, please for God's sake, at least don't you try to teach me what is right and what is wrong." I yell just when Jiju enters the living room, followed by Mom and Dad. When Di was leaving to come here, she also informed Jiju.

"Soni, this is not the way you talk to your elder sister. Go to your room," Mom says, pointing in the direction of my room. When I don't leave, Mom screams, "I said . . . goooooo . . . n-o-w."

Even then I don't leave. I need them to understand me, my position, and my emotions. I am tired of being submissive. I can't give in to everything the way my family wants me to. Some days I have to sacrifice something for Di, zip my mouth and move on. Other days I have to comply with Mom's rules without asking any questions. Sometimes I have to give up on my favorite things so that Girish will stay my best buddy forever, and some days I just walk on the path my dad traces for me. But not anymore. I need to carve my own path. For so long in my life, I have always been obedient, the nice child, sister, student, and even nice person at heart. I am still the same compassionate, courteous person. Loving Esha doesn't change the fact of who I am as a person. I am not going to turn into a merciless, crazy, or bad daughter. What is wrong if I love Esha and want to settle down with her in my life? I want to say, "No, I am not sick. You need to get out of your thinking and see it from my perspective. Love is love. It doesn't confine itself to the boundaries of gender." But I chuck it, knowing nobody would even try to understand me.

"Dad, at least now, you need to understand. She is out of your control. You never trusted my words when I spoke about it. The way it has come out, it's more shameful. This is the time to control her, ban her activities and her liberty," Di says, trying to get Dad into thinking the same way as her.

Mom is certainly on Di's side. But Dad has kept his lips zipped tight since I came back home from my half-finished trip. I can't take it anymore from Di.

I can't believe the way she reacts. She has done many wrong things in her adolescence and I have kept all her secrets with me, except for sharing with Esha in recent times. No one in the family knows about it, not even Girish. The unsaid pressure that I could feel in the house, the stare of our classmates at the trip and the way the board members were looking at both of us is becoming unbearable. On top of all that, Di's actions and provocations are worsening these matters instead of helping us to handle them. Jiju frowns at her to stop, but she ignores him. That is when I reach the limit of tolerating her crap, in spite of me always being her greatest secret keeper and her torture tolerance gadget. As if reading my thoughts, Dad again asks her to calm down before discussing this matter any further. But she ignores Dad too.

But now I lose it.

"Di, enough," I scream right from my belly button.

"You butt out of it. Nobody knows better than me what all you have done with that drug addict boyfriend of yours. That is the real episode of your life, because of which, you got ready to marry someone suddenly."

I never speak up the way I am doing at the moment. Mom foresees an even more intense storm coming before things calm down. She tries to stop me, even tries to drag me toward my room. I don't know when and how I became this fearless. Before leaving the living room with Mom, I turn around and cry it out loud and clear, "Di, you have always tried to talk against me to Mom and Dad, even if I have done only a trivial thing that you didn't like."

"Why don't you tell them today, that you were pregnant with a baby of that boyfriend of yours? The baby that you even aborted without them knowing." That breaks Dad completely. He slaps me and walks away from there. I burst into tears.

Jiju leaves without even asking Di to come with him, but she follows him in tears. And then I run to my room. All of a sudden the silence of the house gives the feeling of loneliness, broken hearts, and perhaps damaged relationships.

*****

Until next morning, Girish and his family are unaware of the chaos that has happened in this household. He too gets mad at me when he comes to know about this incident. He is upset because I assured him I wouldn't take any wrong steps while on our trip, but according to him, I didn't keep my word. He also doesn't talk to me for an entire week after this. Nobody at home talks to me. We don't hear from Di either for a few days.

I miss Esha so much. I want her by my side to lighten my heart and console me. Every minute, I hover around the table in my room, where the phone is located, in a hope to pick up her call, if she calls at all. But she doesn't even try to call. I call on her cell phone a few times; she doesn't pick up. I hope that things aren't as bad at her place as at mine. She gets anxious and nervous really fast. As contradictory as it may sound, she gets scared and panicky equally fast as she spreads the positivity around. I am a bit worried about her.

After a long week—a week that feels like a month or even a year—Mom comes to know from Di that Esha has been going to college. She is not expelled. Not that we didn't know this already. But Di's mentioning it has set the rage back again in the house. I, too, am somewhat angry with her because she doesn't pick up my phone calls anymore. My heart cries thinking I got into a fight with my family for her and she is not even looking back at me. It feels as if time is conspiring to take her far away from me. That thought makes tears roll down my cheek. I barely eat anything for a complete week, but nobody at home cares either, as if my family has already abandoned me. Every single day for hours together, I lock myself in my room to cry it out. This is the worst type of crying I have ever gone through.

Silent crying so that other people in the house don't know about it at all.

Finally, ten days after the incident, Dad talks to me when he receives a letter from college that mentions about a change in the board's decision. They want to reconsider their decision and take me back in college. It seems a few board members have opposed it after the fact. *Wow, quite a mystery*, I think. I am happy that I might go back to college, finish my studies and moreover see Esha.

My joy doesn't last more than a minute. Dad announces calmly and sternly, "I won't send you back to the same college where that girl is going. I don't want you to take this relationship any further. I hope that is clear to you."

"But . . . Dad, for my one mistake, why do I need to compromise with my education?" I ask.

He wraps his one arm around my shoulder and says, "You won't have to compromise with your education. But definitely you have to let go of the liberty I have given you."

I care little at that instant on what he says. Rather, I am relieved by his fatherly gesture. I feel a little less stressed compared to a minute ago. I believe maybe now my family will take care of me. That means a lot. I hold him tight, weep and sob for a long time, till Girish arrives. After exchanging a few words with Girish, Dad goes into the kitchen to talk to Mom. He says to Mom, "I don't feel well. I think I need a walk," and he leaves. I guess, for him walking is the way to relieve the tension. Girish points me to Dad and whispers, "Look at him, at least understand now." followed by a pause.

"By the way, I heard college is ready to take you back. No more expulsion, huh?" he says.

"How in the world do you know about it? Dad just opened the letter a while ago, right in front of me," I wonder.

"Esha called me," he answers. That takes me by surprise. What the heck? Why did she call him and not me?

". . . and?" I demand more information.

Then he shares, "She convinced her dad to talk to the other board members to take you back in college. But in turn her dad took a promise from her."

"Promise! What promise?"

"Her dad took a promise from her to not to talk to you or not to keep any relationship with you at all in college or out of college. That is why she called me and told me to inform you about this."

She also expressed to Girish, "If Soni could finish her B.E. I would be the happiest person. But ask her, please not to approach me in college when she sees me because I won't be able to talk to her. It will be hard for me to ignore her. I hope she understands and helps me in keeping my promise to my dad. Please tell her, I will always love her. The place I have given her in my heart can't ever be replaced by anyone else. But I can't break Dad's promise." He mentions that she hung up the phone crying.

I don't know how to react to this. Should I be happy that she loves me much if she is sacrificing our relationship, just to make sure I could go back to school? Or be sad for being the unluckiest person, for my love leaving me just to get me back to the college? I feel cry rising in my throat again, my eyes become blurry.

Dad comes back from his walk. As if while on the walk he organized the points, which he wanted to mention, in his head. After coming back home, he plainly and loudly announces to me and Mom, "From now on Soni will stay home under observation. She will not be allowed to go out at all. She is grounded from stepping out of the house for three months to start with." He also clarifies that next year I will take admission in a private institute that held an MCA— Master of Computer applications—five years integrated course after the twelfth. For one minute, I feel like just walking out of there. I want to scream at Dad for what he just said. But I can't muster the courage to contend anymore. At last, I put forward my points, but calm and collected, suppressing my anger. "Why can't I go to any other engineering college instead of pursuing an MCA? Please, Dad."

"It is easy to break one's trust. But it takes a lifetime to regain," he replies equally calmly and walks away. But I could see the anger and the disappointment of broken trust behind his still face. Now I wish that I could have learned and practiced being assertive growing up. It may have been completely fine. When I see people around me, I feel everybody gets adapted to how one behaves, how one is. Di has always been stubborn. But, irrespective of whether she has been right or wrong, the family members have adapted themselves according to her. So there is not much pressure on her. But on the other hand, I, being a person who is submissive and defers to the pleasures of others, nobody thinks even once about letting me do what I want to do. They always want to make decisions for me. Or perhaps I am the one who gives in easily.

Even though I don't want to, I give in thinking this behavior might help me win Dad's trust again. Maybe after my graduation, I will find a good job and then earn his blessings for Esha. At that point in time, I will tell him, "See, all this while I walked the path you decided for me. I did everything you said to convince you for Esha. Please Dad!"

Once again, I become the obedient daughter that I have been for years.

On the sly, I weep and sob even more than the last few days. Life has never seemed this meaningless before. Every time I breathe, I hope everything could get back to where it was before the trip. These days, I prefer cutting onions over other domestic work. At least I can let my tears roll down instead of letting them swim, with nobody knowing the real reason for the watering of my eyes. Otherwise, my folks have even started to object to my sobbing for her.

*****

Two Months is a long time for me to stay home without even stepping out for a moment. Actually I am not allowed to go out.

We don't hear from Di as often as before the face off incident. Time is the best healer stands true for Jiju and her. I am happy for them. Jiju accepts the fact, whatever happened between Di and her ex-boyfriend is her past when he didn't even know her. Consequently he moves on to welcome their child—the start of a new life. I hope, at least now, Di will take more care of her family, instead of gossiping around and intruding in other people's life.

After a couple months of confinement within the walls of our house, I want to get back to normal life. Discussing that with Dad helps a bit. That shows his unconditional love for me. I am now allowed to go out, but only with my parents.

I engross myself into my hobby all the time. Every wall of my room ends up having a bunch of paintings. But the more time I spend on painting, the more I miss her.

*****

After a few months, Di and Jiju are blessed with a cute little angel. Di has changed much, mostly for the good. Our relationship gets better day by day, better than ever before, better than I ever imagined. I am thankful to God for Girish being by my side throughout. Whenever I am sad or I miss Esha badly, I talk to him. That lightens me up at least for the time being. The institute where I have joined MCA course, is near Dad's shop. He escorts me every day there and to home after classes are done.

I am tired of being in this confinement built by my parents. No matter how busy I keep my mind, this silly heart and mind of mine, always misses her, a bit more every day, hoping to reunite with her. Little do I realize that this dream of being with her is only a dream—that one has to leave behind when one wakes up.

CHAPTER 16. LIFE SUCKS WITHOUT YOU

Three Years Later
April 2007
Mumbai

ONE FINE SATURDAY MORNING, Di calls and asks Dad to drop me to her house, without even talking to me first. *Why?* I wonder.

The only good thing which has happened, from the fight that Di and I had, the day I came back from the college trip almost three years ago, is that Di has realized her mistake. She took the initiative afterward to come closer to me.

Now we share a strong bond like I have always wished for. Many times, she asks Dad to drop me to her place. Then she takes me out for shopping, movies, hoteling without letting our parents know. They have banned these and other fun activities for me since that incident. Keeping that time aside to take me out is not easy for her, especially now when she is a mom of a tiny tot. She has transformed into a different person altogether. She has stopped most of her bad and annoying habits. Motherhood has changed her into a better person. Now, she empathizes with my pain. The pain of what I am going through. The pain that I carry with me every single moment.

During my childhood and in early youth days, Di and I were never friends. I always felt sad about it. I always felt ashamed of having her as a sister who was nothing but a gossip mill. Nevertheless, I loved her. But in return when I didn't receive affection back, I maintained my distance from her. I am glad that now things, between us, are the way I have always pictured. I am thankful that she is with me today when I really need a friend. The saying, "sisters by fate, friends by choice," now appeals me in every way. Without her support, this time would have been tougher. All this while, she has stood by me as my strength, lifting me up.

Every now and then, she gets updates from Shikha about Esha and then she shares them with me. Once she totally surprised me with a question, "Do you still love her?" When I didn't respond for a few moments, she said, "Your Jiju and I can help convince Mom and Dad after you find your job." I couldn't believe what I heard. Those words truly made me cry and hug her tight.

Dad drops me by Di's. As soon as I come inside, she says, "No matter what it takes, you have to contact Esha today."

"Why, what happened?" I demand, squeezing her arm with a gust of worries storming in my head.

"Shikha told me Esha is getting married in fifteen days to an NRI guy that her parents found for her. She will leave India forever after her final exams."

Suddenly, my heart drops.

I am in tears and yelling, "Why?"

For some reason, I have been hopeful all these years that things would work out in the end. I always thought our love for each other was wonderful and unshakable. I thought after years we would rejoice in love again. But after hearing her news, my heart sinks. I feel a twinge in my heart.

With Di's support, during the last three years, I had called Esha's number many times, but it seemed her number had changed. Shikha didn't have her contact information either. She reported Esha never released that information to anyone. She hardly talked to anyone in the class as if she was under a forced pressure and pain of some kind. She was not allowed to go to any classmate's house and vice versa. She was dropped off at college and picked up from there by her parents in a car, sometimes her mom and sometimes her dad.

There was not a single day when I didn't miss her. Every minute I cried deep down in my heart. I was hoping to have her back in my life someday; maybe after our college graduation or maybe after getting in corporate world.

Truth be told, month after month and year after year I hoped she would contact me. When I couldn't get hold of her and she didn't get in touch with me, whatever hope remained was shrinking smaller day by day. Like a person working strenuously to lose weight loses inches week after week, the same way I was losing hope, bit by bit, to have her back in my life.

Di suggests going to Esha's house as a last option. We both go there, only to learn that they have moved out of that flat two years back. It breaks my already broken heart thousand times over. I cry day and night. To avoid unanswerable questions, I can't let those tears spill out of my eyes in front of my parents. Sometimes I wish my parents would care about my feelings, would understand me better.

"How could she get married to somebody else when I love her the most?" I sob. Didn't she say she loves me too? Suddenly, I feel void and strange. I feel my world of hope is collapsing and I can't do anything about it. I try a lot, but can't get any information on Esha from anywhere. It feels as if she has vanished. Or somebody, perhaps her parents, have hidden her from the world so that I can't be a part of her life any more. A gush of emotions runs through me in a flash. All my emotions hit me hard and make me go weaker. Di even goes to the college to gather information. But the college office refuses to give her information.

There I am, helpless, lost in love . . .

*****

Gradually, hiding a pain with a smile becomes my habit. After making others laugh, letting happy tears roll down becomes my desire. But, no one around me understands; those pretend happy tears are my way of shedding unhappy moans. All of it is to conceal a pain that I carry with me every day.

The thought that she has left me forever is unbearable. I cry the worst kind of cry ever. I want to scream, but can't. I hold my breath to keep quiet. I don't want to breathe anymore because the person who means the most to me is gone . . . far away.

It's entirely my fault, I blame myself.

If I would have stood up for myself, if I wouldn't have been such an obedient daughter as I am, life would have been better. At least I wouldn't have lost Esha forever.

I should have rejoined the college when we received that letter. Why didn't I protest against Dad's decision? I accuse myself a little more.

The hurt caused by love creates a scar that is difficult to heal. After a few days of playing this self-blame game, I decide to heal the scar my own way by doing what I want to, going forward, not letting anyone else make decisions for me anymore.

Di talks to Dad to relax the restrictions on me. She also tells him about Esha's wedding to help him reconsider the ban. That helps.

*****

Two Years Later
June 2009
My graduation day. Dad is super happy that I have been such a good girl these five years of MCA. My parents' unspoken prayer is "Thank God, this girl didn't fall for any other girl in these few years."

I look forward to join the workforce soon. During a campus job fair, I get selected for a job as a Junior Software Developer in a multinational company. First, I will have a few months of training and then I will work on real-time projects for the health care insurance industry.

Every day, on the company bus on my way to work, I daydream about Esha being by my side, working with me in the same office. I also imagine we are both involved in the same project and are sent to another country at the client's office for a few months.

I enjoy the work I do, but not as much as painting. I make a few good friends at work. The more I open myself to other people, the less alone time I find to think about her. My love for her is eternal, though one-sided, I think.

By now, Esha might be all settled in with her husband and might have forgotten about me, I consider. She has not bothered to connect with me. She can never be mine. This is slowly sinking in, a little more every passing day. But I want to do something to make my love immortal. New desire springs within me to satiate my love for her. I want her to know how passionately I loved her. But I don't know how yet. Some ideas are already spinning in my head. I need to give life to one idea that appeals to me the most. The one thing I know for sure though is this time I will not compromise.

CHAPTER 17. LOVE IS IMMORTAL

December 2009
Mumbai

SIX MONTHS INTO MY JOB, I have earned the trust of my colleagues, built strong bond with my teammates and a good rapport with my manager. All of them appreciate my work and are kind to me. My customer is impressed with my efforts. With the speed with which I am learning about the project and taking on new responsibilities, I am hopeful I might get a promotion this coming year. All the appreciation certainly brings out a hidden jealousy among some of my teammates. Every single individual goes through envious experiences at some point in their life. Either a person feels covetous of others or experiences envy from others. The problem arises when one notices and reads it in others' eyes. That is exactly what has happened to me. A few of my teammates have maintained their distance from me since my promotion. As if that were not enough, another bunch takes all the comments I make in an offensive way. These are the times when I figure out who are my true friends.

Krish and Radha, two of my teammates become my close friends. I share my sad story of Esha with them. I see different expressions and gasps on each of their faces when I tell them about us. An awkward glance from Radha that screams from her eyes, "Oh my God, you are gay", makes me stifle a bit. But Krish's question, "When did you first find out that you were … you know, gay?" gives me a chance to mend that awkward feeling that we go through even though for few minutes after Radha's statement. They accept me the way I am. In fact, they promise to help me in my trials and tribulations to form a group to support and help the gay community of Mumbai, which I am planning to form especially for girls. Launching and successfully running this group is my desire to make my love for Esha immortal. But I am not sure how it will all pan out? How I will gather the courage to take such a big step? And above all, how I will keep that big of a secret from a family? Many questions with no answers, but I know one thing for sure, I want to do this for Esha, for us, for many other girls like me out there.

I jot down my action plan and goals. Then I write the steps I will have to take. I understand that I might bump into many blocking stones on my path. But I am prepared. My vision is to start this group to address issues of societal plus family pressure and offer peer support to any lesbian couple who seeks it. I want none other Esha and Soni to have to part their ways.

I know how much I have gone through at home. I am sure Esha might have gone through similar kinds of pressure, which is why she didn't contact me at all. It is good to reach out for help; it is good to share your situation with someone else who could support you through this phase.

I miss having Esha by my side. I think she would be proud of my idea. I know, working on this project with her by my side would have been an altogether different experience. I miss her positive energy, her smile and her bubbly chats. I remember, those positive vibes always helped me during my exam preparations. It also helped me when handling stress given by Di. I am sad that she is not with me today. I think about her and a tear breaks in my eye. Is she still the same person as before, sitting in some other corner of the world? Would her marriage have changed her? Is it possible that she already has kids by now? Then suddenly I muse, *is she already divorced because she might have told her husband about me?* Sometimes I ridicule these thoughts that my mind jumps through within fractions of seconds.

*****

Every evening, I stay late at work. I research on already established gay communities in Mumbai. To my surprise, I find few groups that I never knew. I research them. They focus on raising awareness about the societal and health related problems faced by gay community. They organize various events to reach out to the targeted population. I note down the names and contacts of the existing groups and communities.

One by one I call most of them. Unfortunately, they all go to voicemail. I leave them a voice message and a call back number, but I don't hear from any of them.

The next couple of months at work are crazy busy. Our U.S. client is demanding and asks the team to complete the project before agreed-upon time. It adds massive pressure on the entire team. Everyone is asked to work day and night. I stay late every evening to finish my office work. The entire team works hard. This is the time when the bond between Krish, Radha, and I gets stronger. Cracking jokes with each other, pulling each other's leg, complaining about things and laughing out loud while we are stressed and tired, is comforting. They both are great to work with. Work combined with a hint of fun gives the perfect kick to our project. In these past two months, our manager has ordered different cuisine for the team staying late. The first few days he ordered without asking us. Gradually the team submits their requests for food they want to try.

By the time we leave work, we are dead tired. The shuttle service is provided by the company for late commutes. Many times, we fall asleep on our way home. In part, this is made possible thanks to Radha's strange condition. She can't sleep while traveling; it doesn't matter if she travels by train, plane, car, or any other vehicle. She gets hyper when in motion hence she can't sleep. I had heard of motion sickness in the past, but never heard of motion anxiety. However, this works to our advantage. She wakes everyone up once we reach our stops. A couple of months slip by getting no more work done for the support group I want to create.

Once the office project is delivered, tested, and approved by the customer, we get a breathing room. I jump onto my tasks again. I restart making phone calls one more time in the hope somebody will pick up. Finally, lady luck knocks my door; I hear a voice on the other end. I hold my excitement and pitch my idea in nice words. The person on the other line firsts listens intently then in few words says, "That sounds like a good idea. I definitely want to know more." I get a chance, an opportunity to meet one of the leading gay organizations' head.

*****

Thursday evening, after work I leave to meet the head of that organization. Krish accompanies me. I had insisted he come with me; I don't know why but I felt a bit nervous going there by myself. As we enter the elevator, the liftman salutes "Salam Saheb—hello sir" and asks what floor, looking at Krish, who is busy texting. When I say five, he stares a little and says in his hoarse voice, "I tell no one. Who comes, who leaves? Are you here to get help from them?" Then pointing towards Krish, liftman asks, "Who is he, your brother?" When I give him a harsh look of will you stop asking me questions, he immediately changes the topic to Mr. Shah. "Mr. Shah is a nice and simple man. I have been the liftman in this building for the last six years. He supports my kids school expenses too."

"That is nice of him," Krish responds, turning off his phone. We reach floor five and I heave a sigh of relief as I come out of the elevator. Krish rolls his eyes at me, hinting that the liftman babbles too much.

As we reach the office, the receptionist takes us to Mr. Shah's cubicle. One more time I narrate the story. It feels as if every time I tell it, I re-live the dreadful moment when our secret came out. It feels as if I still suffocate from the thoughts of the time that added sadness and darkness to my life. After hearing it, Mr. Shah says, "I know, what has happened with you is sad and unfortunate. I understand it might feel like the end of the world to you. But trust me you are fortunate; I have heard more dreadful stories. We are here to help in any way we can."

I listen to Mr. Shah quietly and nod. His is a thinly framed body, and he has dark brown eyes that reveal his enthusiasm and passion for his work. He wears a mix of black and gray hair combed back, looking shiny as if he had just gotten a hair oil massage before coming to the office. He shares with us what his organization does, the events they run and workshops they organize to spread awareness. The way he speaks about his organization shows his passion equally well.

He also encourages me to meet with other groups and clubs; which I have already read about online. At last he says, "Let us know if we can help you in any way." He takes a visiting card out of his pocket and hands it over to me.

Instantly I realize he stopped the conversation by handing over his visiting card. But I haven't even shared my idea of the support group with him yet. I don't want to lose an opportunity to at least mention it. So I steer the conversation to thank him for his valuable time and then say, "I read about what you have gone through to build this organization. I salute you for that. It is incredible what you have done and continue to do. You have a huge fan right here in front of you." Then I see a smile again. "And I mean it," I emphasize. The best thing relating to him is he doesn't stir even a bit in reaction to much praise from me. I share my idea of establishing a group to help discuss societal and family pressure for girls in a relationship.

To my points, he instantly adds, "Not only societal and family pressure; there is a bunch of other issues to discuss along with it. We can add a counseling unit along those lines."

Oh, he likes my idea. I do a little jig in my head.

After discussing further details with him about my idea, we commit to meet again.

*****

Mr. Shah, his entire team and I discuss the contents of what should go in the support group proposal. After a long, productive two hour meeting; we take away our to-dos.

Few weeks later we meet again. This time with a written proposal document. The team has done a wonderful job of laying out the proposal. An impressive executive summary write up, followed by statement of need and anticipated benefits, goals for next two years and also the answers to a few frequently asked questions are included in the document. Few minor refinements and we are good to go.

Before involving the financial supporters, a prep meeting is held with Mr. Shah, Mr. Mehta (public relation officer), the head of Diversity Leadership Committee, a team of counselors from Mr. Shah's organization and I. As Mr. Mehta briefs us on the initiative, I secretly feel proud of myself. I am also surprised to know from these meeting that LGBT individuals struggle with higher occurrences of depression and suicidal thoughts, which have been linked to personal experiences involving harassment, discrimination, interpersonal conflict and lack of social supports. Several of them feel isolated once family and friends seclude them after they find out about it; Esha and I are a live example of that. This support center will provide these girls backing they lack today. It will assist them in their personal growth and confidence to stand up as a LGBT person. Few questions are asked specifically to me on how the idea of this group popped up in my head. I reiterate my story to leave few of them teary eyed.

Soon a final meeting invite is sent out to the fund sponsors – some include Mr. Shah's existing fund sponsors and a few that he gathered through his extensive networking.

*****

After several weeks, the day of meeting is finally here. I am nervous before the meeting. Secretly, I hope and pray that everything goes well. This is a formal meeting. We all are dressed in proper formal work attire for it. I take a day off from my job to attend this meeting. In the meeting, Mr. Mehta presents the high level information as planned. He plans to head this initiative himself since his subordinates can handle the matters of other group now. I will assist Mr. Mehta and Mr. Shah until I am comfortable running this group myself. Mr. Shah continues the meeting by providing more details about the plan. This entire process is a huge learning experience for me. I have jumped into this unknown territory on impulse, but now I feel, it wouldn't have been possible without Mr. Shah's team. It is a lot of work to form a support group, way bigger effort than I have ever imagined. But I am glad at last everything falls in place. Meeting went really well, and we got support from two sponsors - one a private organization and other a government lobbying agency.

We continue meeting weekly, arrange successful events every month, work together hour after hour; my goal seems closer now.

*****

Throughout the journey of getting this group set up, I miss her a lot. Even though she can't be with me ever again, I imagine her being by my side. If I get stuck somewhere, I picture her in my mind, what she would say if she would be in this situation. I end up doing what I think she would do. It seems as if I still live my life with her in my own little world that is limited only to my thoughts. I cherish the good times we spent together. But I hate our parting, rather she leaving me. Without her, nothing is the same. A sunny day doesn't bring sunshine on my face anymore. Beats of songs don't make me dance anymore. Traveling in an auto rickshaw without her has become boring, dull, and mundane. I miss how she used to crack jokes, and then deliberately jab her elbow in my arm to make me laugh on her jokes. Even drinking lassi, I don't enjoy anymore. It reminds me of her; it reminds me of the good times that will never return. Sometimes I feel, without her, my life has become an empty box with a giant hole in it. A box that is good for nothing anymore. But life has to move on; that is what everybody around me says.

Then unexpectedly I feel resentment for her brewing up in me. The resentment comes because she is not here with me anymore. *She left me. She didn't stick by the promises she gave me. She didn't put me above her other relationships in life, unlike me, always putting her on the top. I fought with Di. I even had cold wars and differences with Girish just for her. I even fought with my dad for her. Her love gave me courage to stand up for myself. It taught me to speak up for things I desired rather than just giving in to the wishes of my loved ones. But when she left me, I saw no other way to handle anything than being a timid puppet again. A puppet who dances to the strings of what her owners decide. Exactly, the same way as I followed and did everything that my parents decided for me.*

I feel motivation and hope for love is gone from my life forever. The only thing remaining in me is resentment and then some more resentment. I never imagined that our relationship would be doomed like this.

*****

I am impressed with the way Mr. Shah executes my idea and brings it to life. He builds the whole team for supporting the group. He convinces the lobby of the government to fund our project. I am surprised to see how many people out there are supportive and ready to volunteer. All this is possible only because of Mr. Shah. The way he has dedicated himself to this purpose is beyond comparison. Without his guidance and support, my idea would have remained merely a thought scribbled on a piece of paper. It is kind of him to offer premises and technical support to operate 'Madadgar' - meaning Supporter, Helper. Yes, Madadgar is the name of the group. It takes almost a year and two months to complete the legwork. The date for the launch of the group is decided. Two more months—the thought of it makes my stomach feel funny. On my way home, I practice in my head how and what I will say to Di,

Jiju, and Girish. I don't know how they will react to my work that I have been doing secretly after office hours. But I can't wait till tomorrow to go to Di's to talk about this.

*****

February 2011

After many months of hectic schedule, I spend Saturday with Di, Jiju, Girish, and our darling Riya. Food is catered from outside. All we do is eat and have fun. With Riya's giggling and crying music alternating in the background, a card game sets the mood of the evening. After a few games of Bluff, we take a break from card games. Di puts our princess to bed. We four sit and laze in the four different corners of two sofas. We chat over random things. I grab the chance and talk about my secret project of forming lesbian help group. At first they are stunned. The next moment, two pillows are thrown at me from different directions because I didn't share this with them for a long time. Catching those pillows and sticking my tongue out, I say, "Sorry."

Immediately the next question arises on how and when I will share about my secret project with Mom and Dad. Would they approve of it? I truly feel good the way Di and Girish treat me like an adult now. They let me make my own choices, no questions raised, and no looks given at all. I wish Mom and Dad would do the same. "I think tomorrow," I reply, hiding the insecurities bubbling up in my mind. Insecurities of how Dad will react to this. Will he bring out other ways of shutting me down? But on the other hand, I am not worried about whether they will approve of me being part of Madadgar. If I am there or not, Madadgar will be born in two months. It will go live.

*****

Sunday Morning

I talk to Dad and Mom regarding the work I have been doing during evening hours. I start the conversation like this, "I know there are certain things that you both don't approve of who I am."

Mom interrupts, "If we are talking about her again, please stop right here."

I retort, "You both need to hear me out, please, just once. And Mom, it is not about her. It is relating to me. It is about the work I have been doing on the side after my office work. First and foremost, I apologize that I lied to you guys. I didn't work in the office after hours late every evening." Then I tell them everything. I share with them about the group that will be launched in two months. I also share with them that this was my idea and how this is turning into reality. I tell them about Mr. Shah.

Mom gets a little hyper and stands up to blurt while I am done telling only a part of it. Dad holds her hand and without saying anything he asks her to sit down, just with an eye gesture. By the time I finish talking, Mom is in tears. But she says nothing as opposed to how she would always overreact to things a few years back. It feels as though with age she is getting tired of the problems and tensions I have created for them. As usual Dad doesn't react. All he says is, "Work on finishing it. But just make sure, your name is not related to that group in any way. We don't want it in print on any document or any other media. And also make sure you don't go for the launch."

Then he stands up. I look at his face. Wrinkles have made their way around his big eyes. I see a tassel of white hair in his right eyebrow. The skin around his neck has sagged a little. I notice hunch of his back when he says in a soft but stern voice, "In this country, for middle-class people like us, it is impractical and impossible to settle down with the same gender partner. Finish the work for the group, but then I am marrying you off to a boy." That's all. Then he leaves. I am shocked. Neither one of them reacted. Seems age is catching up with him. I didn't realize it earlier. It feels as if I am making him age faster. The rest of the day, I ponder over what Dad said. Di and Girish also mentioned the same point a few times lately. I agree with them; they are not wrong.

The thought of getting married to a boy makes me want to run away. But I can't cause any more grief to my parents. I have already given them white hairs way before their time. Moreover, if I can't spend the rest of my life with Esha, it doesn't matter who else I spend my life with. I convince myself to submit to an arranged marriage. This will be an arrangement that Dad and my family make for me. I bury my love for her in my heart as a seed of immortality and reach decision to move on.

CHAPTER 18. TIE THE KNOT

DEEP IN MY HEART I know I can't love any other person in my life than Esha. So If I have to compromise in any situation, I might as well make my parents happy. I know it will be a hell of a difficult marriage for me, but it really doesn't matter anymore since she left me.

Girish suggests that if I want to marry Abhay, he is still very much interested.

He says, "Abhay realizes that Esha is a closed chapter of your life now."

I have seen no one else as crazy in love as him; I wow him in my head.

But I don't want to marry Abhay. I believe he deserves someone better than me. I don't want to be the reason to hurt him in any way. I am not sure if I will survive the marriage, the whole lifetime with any guy. I am really not sure.

Per Dad's wish, I talk to Mr. Shah to make sure to not print my name anywhere. I am grateful to him that he has given life to my idea. He has a strong group. I wish I could continue to be part of the Madadgar family. But I want to avoid any more grievances to my parents by going against them. Secretly, I may be in touch with the group.

Mom and Dad look for some potential grooms for me. Unlike what my family may have expected, I find it an unexciting and lame job to look at those groom pictures. Most of them are NRIs living either in the USA or UK. The photographs are characterized by nerdy expressions and attention poses. I haven't found one that has captivated me yet. Even though it is a boring task, sometimes, after looking at some guy's bug-eyed, glazed, straight-faced, and vacant expressions in the pictures, I have hysterical laughter attacks throughout the day. Not only photographs, I am also given a profile summary of many boys to read. The criterion to pass on the selected profile summary to me is simple. If my parents like his qualifications and he is an NRI, then they look at his picture. If he is decent looking, all the information—bio-data of a boy, they call it—is handed over to me for my review. Some guys have a funny profile summary. I can't stop laughing when I read it.

One has what I think of as the "OK-Syndrome." He uses OK in each and every sentence of his profile summary. It reads as I quote below:

"I am a down-to-earth guy who is outgoing and has a great personality OK. I love to laugh and enjoy great company OK. I consider myself humble and modest OK. So I am looking for a life partner OK. A girl should love to laugh with me OK. If you think you are humble, modest and would love to laugh with me, contact me OK!"

"I definitely don't want to marry this guy, OK," I say out loud putting his bio-data aside.

There is one more. He has a few lines of description about himself in his profile summary that we found online. The way he describes himself, I want to read and know more about him. But toward the end of the summary he writes, "I am looking for a life partner who would understand me better than I understand myself." What a demand! Then it continues, "She should be able to adjust with me forever." All I can think in my head is, really? It doesn't stop there. "She should never create any difficulties in my life or in her life. That way the entire life can run smoothly and easily." These last two lines make me go crazy. I hold my stomach, hurting from unstoppable laugh and hear myself saying out aloud, "Wow, what a way to run a life smoothly!"

Mom and Dad go through profiles of many potential grooms. Some they don't like, a few Di doesn't, and others don't like me. While groom hunt process goes on, many times I sway from my decision, but I keep it to myself only. But one fine day, I decide that going forward I won't ponder over my past at all. I have two choices. Either I dwell in my past, staying right where I am today, being afraid of moving forward and assuming the worst is yet to come. Or I move on, leaving the past behind, assuming the unknown in front of me will be exceptionally bright and brilliant. Just like Esha once decided and never looked back at me. In the same way, I will move on with my life. I will rejuvenate myself into a new girl, I believe. Then, silently and softly, I affirm to myself, "I will always try to stick to the decision I am making today and be happy as much as I can."

In a week, I meet an NRI, Rajeev. My parents find him through a matrimonial site. At present, he is in India on a bride hunt. His parents also live in Mumbai. Everybody at home likes him. But Di, Jiju, and Girish are being proactive. They stand by me, telling Dad, "Though we like him, if Soni says no, nobody should force her." Mom and Dad agree with them.

After a few meetings with Rajeev, I am flattered by his charming personality. I feel comfortable being in his company. But, I am not sure yet, if I want to marry him. In spite of the many promises that I made to myself, I find it difficult to take that next step. I find it hard to move on. I cry and pray to God for a miracle to happen. I pray God to send Esha back in my life. But in my life, nothing happens according to my wish. Sometimes my parents don't want to honor my wish and sometimes God is not pleased with me. The time that I spent with Esha, the special, intimate moments that I shared with her, again flash in front of me as if to hold me back from getting married to this guy. I try to turn off that part of my memory for a while. I wish I had a switch to turn those thoughts off. Possibly, this signals a research opportunity for a scientist somewhere, to make a pill where people can erase specific memories they have had.

After meeting him for the third time today, I sit in my room looking out the window. Staring at the Flyover Bridge, which connects Mulund East to West. I stare at all the autos and taxis to capture the scene in my memory as if I won't be back ever again. My mind is not in the state to think. How can one decide assertively to marry someone without knowing enough about that person? I find it to be a daunting task. Nobody in this wide world is sure of what lies in the future for them. Neither am I. I am definitely nervous to get married to an unknown person. Scary thoughts force me to give up. Many what ifs are crossing my mind. What if he is just being nice and charming now? In reality, what if he is not as caring as he presents himself now? My chain of what if's breaks when Mom and Dad enter the room. They both sit next to me.

Mom demands, "What do you think about him?"

I am still thinking should I marry him or should I not. I am not ready to reply yet.

She continues, "Beta, we won't say yes to them or force you if you don't like him. But let us know what you think about him. At least talk to us anything, something regarding him."

Good lord, you guys should not have forced me almost eight years ago to follow your decision of not sending me to the same college as Esha, I want to say, but I keep quiet reminding myself of my decision to not reflect on the past.

"May be . . . maybe I like him," I reply hesitantly.

"You don't seem sure yet. Do you like him like him or just like him?" Dad questions in a soft but firm tone. I don't know why dads always need firm answers from their daughters for everything.

After a silence of few seconds, I assure, "Dad, I like him."

*****

Suddenly everybody in the house is cheerful. Preparations for the wedding are in full swing.

One last time I go to Mr. Shah's office. I meet him and his entire Madadgar team. The Madadgar group has been launched successfully. The number of girls contacting them for help is unbelievable. All the surprising facts are coming out as never before.

I can't believe, in a few days, I will get married and fly to the United States. The visa appointment is all arranged. Di instructs me on how to be a nice wife and daughter-in-law. I am somewhat sad to leave India and go to another country. I am sad that I won't be able to spend much time with Girish and Di going forward. She gives me her makeup wish lists to buy for her from there when I come to India next time. She says teasing me, "You won't have time to look at my list after the wedding. That is why I am giving you the list now." Her eyes display naughtiness like a teenager.

I find it difficult to accept that I am getting married to someone other than Esha. We had to part our ways against my wish. She walked away just like that even without saying goodbye. Her walking away was a painful way to convey "I love you." I try to forget her and the time I spent with her. But that seems next to impossible. I try to bury her deep in my memories so that thoughts of her don't rise to make me sad and discourage me from my decision of getting married to Rajeev. I try hard to not bow in sadness. I finally loosen my clutch on the past and let go of her thoughts and memories. I embrace the present. I bring a smile on my face, initially forcibly. But slowly, I find myself getting lost among the happiness of my family.

Many families and friends attend the wedding. I see some happy and some sad eyes around me that day. I see the pain in Abhay's eyes, the same kind of pain as I went through when Esha got married. The only difference is he can talk to me whenever he wants to, but she never gave me that chance. By marrying Rajeev, I enter a new world. I will move to New Jersey with him to start a new life. I pretend to forget whatever happened in the past. I consider this marriage as an opportunity to have a fresh start to my life. It is a new day, a new start, and the beginning of a new phase of my life. I enter a whole new world with tons of aspirations to live happily ever after.

CHAPTER 19. A NEW WORLD

May 2012
New Jersey
Present Day

SEEING ESHA TODAY IN THE MALL, my past life has come haunting me again. Suddenly, my urge to get the answers from her has reached its zenith. The thoughts of her shatter me completely from inside out as if I were living those years one more time. Forgetting that past was difficult, but now when I recall it, it's worse to run through it all over again. All those moments of us being together, getting separated, and my craving for her are flashing back. In this last year, I have always thought, my memories of her are fading; my feelings for her are changing. But all that seems wrong today. She is still alive in my heart somewhere. Many times when Rajeev has been at work, sitting alone I used to miss her, but not enough to stir me. Now, replaying her smiles and giggles breaks me to pieces, leaving me lonely one more time. I sense a strong desire to see her and be with her again.

The phone rings; I don't pick it up. After ignoring it a few times, it rings once again. I pick up this time, with quivering hands. With a shaky voice, I say "Hello." It's Girish on the line. He shares the news of his upcoming wedding. He is getting married to his girlfriend of a few years now. When he doesn't hear the cheer in my voice as he expected, especially after breaking the news, he asks what is wrong. I break into a shriek, saying, "I saw her."

After a few seconds of silence, I cry out loud and ask him, "Why again? Why?"

Not knowing what to say, he remains inaudible. He lets me cry. Putting the phone down, I cry more. I cry for many hours till my tears finally dry.

When I pull myself together and think about how to contact Esha, I realize I don't have any information to get in touch with her. I jump on the computer. I Google her but find nothing. I also search by her name on Facebook, but no luck. Trying to contemplate what my options are, I call my Di. But cannot get hold of her at that minute. Before getting married to Rajeev, I had decided not to regret my decision and just be happy. But, then I never considered what if I see her again in front of me. I wish I could talk to Di right now.

The entire day and evening, I spend sitting on the sofa, without having a bite, only drenching myself in old memories; the shadow of which does not stop to follow me. I try to soothe my heart, the toughest job of my life. I try not to let my thoughts wander to those old times spent with her. I pick cooking to divert my mind. I cook food for Rajeev as he might come home soon and if food is not ready, he will literally get mad beyond imagination. In the past, whenever I didn't cook food before his arrival, he got upset and said mean words to me. He needles me about the housework I do. He raises his voice at me often. When he arrives home, if food is not ready, it ticks him off. If he notices a small crease in his office shirt that I ironed for him, he yells and makes me re-iron it while he bursts my ears with his screeching. He repeats these jibes so often that sometimes I believe I am the dumb one, in this house, who can't do a single job skillfully without getting screamed at. This stimulates my already impelling urge to find a job, a kind that I enjoy instead of one I am forced into. But having an H4 visa ruins my prospects. I pray and hope that our green card comes as soon as it can. Rajeev's green card process has been started since early 2005. Last year when we got married, he applied for adjustment of status to combine me in his green card application. Lately, Rajeev once mentioned that we are close to getting our permanent residency. I hope we get it soon.

He has many habits which I loathe. I wish I could change those. I don't like that his work always takes significance and precedence over everything else in his life. But the one thing that I hate the most about him is him sharing all bits and pieces of our bedroom life with his mom. That is too much for me to digest without getting mad at him. Initially, I kept quiet, thinking this mumma's boy would change with time. But, nothing has changed in a year. When I always want to be the first one to know his news of all kinds, his mom is the one who gets it first "always". Should I dare to complain about his behavior, he doesn't stop himself from saying, "I may not be right in what I do, but you are more wrong here. You want to know why? Because you are jealous. Unlike you, I share a special bond and a close relationship with my mom." His harsh tone and words pierce every inch of my heart. As a result, if I break down and cry, he tells me, "Way too sensitive of a person you are! I said nothing that should hurt you or make you sob like this."

Sometimes I never know what to expect when he comes home. Every evening brings uncertainty with it. Every time I see the sun setting, a thought crosses my mind; *will today bring loving and caring Rajeev at the door with something nice in his hand to surprise me? Or will Rajeev who is high with his rage and who threatens me with his harsh words and strong actions be home today?* Even though he shows his care for me when in a good mood, many times small things trip him badly. As a result, he explodes his anger by occasionally hitting me. At other times, he relieves himself by forcing me to do things I would rather not and eventually by forcing himself on me if I say no.

*****

13 May 2012
Our first wedding anniversary

Surprisingly, Rajeev wakes up early in the morning, before me. Usually I am the one waking him up every day, but today is different. He is up early. I sit on the bed yawning. He sits next to me. Moving aside my hair gently, he lands a kiss on my neck. He hugs me and whispers in my ear, "Happy Anniversary Honey!"

Wow, very romantic for a change. Such a happy start to one more year of married life that sucks, I think without saying a word. Is everything OK with him? Never in the last year, especially on any weekday's morning, has he shown any romantic gesture because he is always in a rush to go to the office.

Typically he returns late and leaves early for the office. Most of the time, he eats lunch at his work cafeteria. Mostly, I am alone at home to do household chores. He even doesn't have time to teach me how to drive. For me this year has been kind of jail in this house. I only get to go out when Rajeev wishes, other than to the supermarket where I go by city bus for grocery shopping.

They say the first year of marriage is a blissful time for a couple. Unfortunately, I haven't experienced that.

For the entire last year he has always been neck deep in his work. Work has always been the first and top priority for him when I should have been at least as a newlywed. I complained about it few times, but those complain irritated him. So I stopped complaining. This whole last year, I have always been forced to live up to his expectations, always giving only, either by wish or by force.

I turn around to look at him, "Thank you, Happy Anniversary to you too!" I wish him and cuddle him still thinking about Esha.

I force my mind not to contemplate about Esha, but rather enjoy the rare moment with him. Since the last few weeks, when I saw her at the mall, I have been trying to be an even better wife every day. I am trying to convince my heart to go back to caring about Rajeev. But it seems, this silly soul doesn't want to understand that. Rather, one more time now it's falling for her. That scares me.

I brush my teeth and then enter the kitchen to make tea. Before entering the kitchen, I see something on the dining table that surprises me.

Why is he showering so much love on me suddenly? I wonder.

Nevertheless I enjoy it. Somewhat oddly, a bouquet of orange roses is waiting on the table for me to notice. It's sweet of him to remember that I love orange roses. For a wee minute, I am happy.

I embrace him again, saying, "Now I know why you were awake before me this morning." But this nice gesture doesn't make me forget the emotional scars he has given me in the past year. I let go of the clutch.

When I walk to the kitchen, holding my hand to stop me from going, he says, "Sonia, take a look at something else too. This is for both of us."

He takes an envelope from under the vase of rose flowers. I was so excited seeing the flowers that I missed it. He handed the envelope to me. It holds two tickets for a cruise liner vacation to the Bahamas. I am animated, dancing and whistling. I can't thank him enough for this lovely surprise. With Rajeev's busy work schedule, we haven't been out on any vacation in the entire last year. We even skipped the honeymoon. I am super eager to go somewhere to have fun and relax time. It might give both of us chance to connect with each other more.

In excitement, I don't even look at the dates on the tickets and shoot out a question at him, "Are we leaving tonight?" I think it's our anniversary, so we might leave tonight to celebrate it.

He replies, "Umm . . . you know I really need to finish my current assignment and only then can we go. My current assignments' product goes live on July fifteenth. After that, two more weeks of client support and then I am done with this assignment. Keeping assignment timeline in mind, I booked tickets to Florida for August second. We sail from there on third August." That blows off my excitement balloon. Two and half more months are a long way to go.

I force a smile to hide my sad-looking face and turn to the kitchen. Then I say, going toward the stove, "I understand."

But truth to be told, I don't want to understand it today. I am tired of understanding his love for work. I am tired of being his second priority always. Not once, has he made me feel special by making me his first priority. But I don't want to say it out loud at this moment. The few times whenever I showed that concern, we ended up in a fight.

"Do you want me to leave my work and sit home with you? Who will feed you then?" he had asked in the harsh and angry tone. Then he continued with fury, "What's your problem? You always have complaints. Sometimes you don't like me sharing anything with my mom; sometimes you don't like me spending that extra hour or two at work. What do you like then? Can't you appreciate any single thing about me?"

After having tea and breakfast, he gets ready for the office and leaves at around 7:45 AM. I don't know why, but I don't enjoy today's tea, even though I made it exactly the same as always. Possibly I am too upset to make good tea or maybe too upset to drink it, I consider.

Once he leaves for the office, I continue with my everyday routine. Today I feel a little weird. I am lazy, nauseous and woozy. I want to lie down. But I don't. I have lots to finish. I plan to cook a special dinner for tonight. Malai kofta, chicken biryani, chapatti, and rasmalai are on the menu for tonight. To cook these dishes, then clean the house followed by setting the dinner on the table, will surely take a lot of time. I also have to buy a nice card for him. I can't afford to rest.

*****

The food is ready before noon. I keep working till I get hungry. My growling tummy says chicken biryani will do well. But I tell myself not to eat. I don't feel like eating chicken. Then I consider, maybe malai kofta with leftover chapatti, is the better choice. Otherwise I love malai kofta, but today I don't want to eat it either. I end up having a bowl of fruits, which is not my usual preference. *Is anything wrong with me today?* I ask myself.

My talk with myself is interrupted by the phone ringing.

"Hi Mom," I say after I hear Mom from the other end of the phone.

"Hi Beta, Happy Anniversary! How are you? How is Rajeev?"

"We both are well. He went to the office. We will take a cruise vacation. He gifted me a vacation package on our anniversary today," I express excitedly. That doesn't make my mom happy. Instead she is sad and asks, "What? He didn't gift you any jewelry," (long pause; she waits for my reply, I don't reply, so she continues), "really, he did not?" I hear disappointment and worry in her voice.

To avoid the topic of the least interest to me, I say, "Leave it, Mom. You tell me, how are you? Where is Dad? Is he not home yet?"

"No he is at the shop. Nowadays he comes home late, working really hard. Did you eat lunch?" Moms are always worried about your eating whether you eat or you don't.

"Did you eat enough? If you don't eat well, you will lose weight. If that happens, people will say you are not happy with your husband so you are dropping off weight." I repeat it in my mind the way she always says. But then I realize, in fact I haven't eaten much today since morning.

"Mumma, I didn't want to eat any food. I ate one apple and two oranges."

"You never liked apples. Good! You are eating it now. It's good for your health," she emphasizes, followed by seconds of hush. Then she investigates, "Do you feel nauseated at all?"

"Mom, you are too much. No, I don't think I am pregnant," I protest hastily.

"Still, go to the doctor today. You never listen. This time you have to. Call me tomorrow for sure to tell me about it."

"OK, I will. Bye now," and I hang up. I get annoyed at Mom for suggesting that I am pregnant. But on second thought, I always loved malai kofta. Then how come I couldn't eat it today? Maybe I am pregnant.

One after another I receive calls from Girish, Di–Jiju, and then Dad. It feels wonderful to hear them wish me enthusiastically. I miss them a lot. I wish to visit them as soon as possible. It's been almost a year I haven't seen them. We virtually see each other through Skype. But it doesn't have the charm of an in-person meeting.

After tending these calls, I clean the house. Then I wash the dishes and take a shower. I eat more fruits before going out as I get hungry again.

*****

I board the bus that comes two blocks away from our apartment to go to the nearby supercenter. On the bus, at the next stop, a lady sits next to me. She has a cute baby, around ten months old, on her lap. The baby smiles at me when I make funny faces for her. I see a few familiar faces on the bus from our neighborhood. An elderly couple who lives in the same apartment complex as us exchanges a gentle smile with me. Many times when I go grocery shopping, I have seen them in the same bus. Getting off at my regular stop, I spend some time in a shop looking for the right card. Then I buy a couple beautiful candles. Those candles remind me of Esha again. When we were on our college trip, she mentioned how much she loved candles. She also expressed what she dreamt for our first date. She said whenever we would have our first official date; she would be the person in charge of the arrangements. Sky would be our roof. In the presence of shiny stars and brightly lit moon with bunch of candles surrounding us, I would kiss you to eternity my love.

 After buying candles, when I am moving toward the checkout counters, I see the Health Beauty Care aisle. I am tempted to go through that aisle to look at makeup products. During my two years of a corporate job, I got into the habit of wearing makeup. Di is a pro at it. So I didn't face much of a problem learning how to apply it. She helped me a lot. While passing through that lane, my eyes read the label of a pregnancy test kit sitting right there on the shelf.

Let's buy it, my mind says at once.

No. No, you don't need it. You are not pregnant, comes another thought.

Did I miss my period this month? Yes, I think so. I am fifteen days overdue for my period, I say to myself. My periods have been quite irregular lately, so I couldn't say for sure if missed periods are because of irregularity or something else?

*****

As soon as I enter the house, the clock that is ticking on the wall opposite to the entry door shows the time 4:50 PM. I still have enough time before Rajeev comes home at 6:00 if he comes home a few hours earlier as decided in the morning. My anxiety, to know if I am pregnant, reaches a peak. I leave the shopping bags on the dining table and grab the pregnancy test kit. Then I run to the bathroom; 1, 2, 3, 4, 5, 6, 7, 8, 9 . . . the color turns pink. I can't believe how fast it turned pink. So I use the other strip too. Each kit has two test strips, now I get it why two. Again pink. "Crap!" That is the first word I hear my mind screaming. And, then a gentle and happy smile.

CHAPTER 20. ALONE SOME

MY JAW DROPS, and happy tears make their way out of my eyes. "Happiness is about to begin," I hear saying it in my head. I feel magical. I feel delighted, so content, but don't know how to react. In seconds, I dream of the life ahead of me with my kid and Rajeev. One more time I promise my heart to let go of Esha's memories, this time forever. I can definitely do that for the betterment of my child.

In a few minutes, I come out of the bathroom. Looking at the clock again, I work hard to organize everything in a perfect manner. I want to make this evening remarkable for both of us. I organize the dishes in proper places, and then I clean the dining table. I set up the food and the flower bouquet that he brought for me. I arrange candles all over the dining table and last but not the least, I place the card which I purchased from the supermarket, on the table next to the flowers.

In a jiffy, I am ready and dressed up. Dark pink and green kurti with pink legging, a hint of nude lip gloss, along with earrings of a gold and green combination, completes my getup. After coming to the USA, I hardly get to wear fancy Indian dresses. At home I am more comfortable in my jeans and T-shirt.

Sitting next to the window watching all the cars coming home, keeping my hands over my tummy, I talk to my baby. "Sweetie, Dad will be home any time. He will be happy to know about you."

I feel as if mom-baby bonding, a world of togetherness, has begun. It is already part of my life now since the last hour. This new angel has no existence in the outside world yet, but the feeling of its presence inside me redefines my world in seconds. I never imagined how it would be to have a life—a creature of God—inside me. A thought crosses my mind, *Life is tough enough, but this is for sure going to be wonderful.*

As soon as I see from the living room window, the black Honda Accord that Rajeev is parking, a cold wind whirls around me. Suddenly, I am nervous to share the news of my pregnancy with him rather than being happy.

"Silly, he will be happy. This is the best gift ever," I mutter, trying to cheer myself to reduce a sudden nervousness.

Even before I can open the door, he opens it with his set of keys. He places the office bag on the table positioned near the entrance door. He stares at me in surprise.

"Somebody is looking gorgeous today," he praises while walking through living room. He comes closer to embrace me.

"That somebody is also super happy today," I say, cuddling him and landing a peck on his cheek.

He holds my chin and pushes it up in a gentle way. Then, looking into my eyes, he affirms, "Yes, I can see that somebody is delighted. Tell tell . . . why why? What is the secret?"

"I won't tell you that easily. Go get freshened up, we will have dinner first," I say, pushing him to the bathroom.

I take out the chocolate pastry, which I brought from the store earlier today, from the fridge and set it on the dining table amidst the rest of the things. I place one candle next to the pastry.

"Come quickly, I have been waiting for you . . . I am hungry now," I scream, looking at the bedroom. And then I light the candle.

"Wow! Why did you cook this much? We could have gone out for dinner," he states looking at the food that is arranged on the dining table. He says it in a way as if he doesn't mean it. But again, I know he loves Indian food and the dishes on the table are a few of his favorites.

We cut the pastry. Showering me with a few kisses, he feeds me a bite of pastry. He notices the greeting card that is propped in front of the flower vase. Licking the chocolate cream off his fingers, he picks up the card with his salivated fingers and reads it.

Baby,

I ❤ you. Wish you happy first Wedding Anniversary and many more!!

Well, I didn't buy any gift for you. But on our first anniversary, I have the best gift to give you. Wait to know what it is.

Tick tick 60 . . . tick tick 59 . . . tick tick 58 . . . after a short dinner break.

Luv you,

Me

He wraps his arms around me and says, winking at me, "I already know the gift you are referring to. I can't wait."

Coming closer and looking in my eyes, he says playfully, "Didn't we just eat pastry? I am full now. How about I get the gift first and then we eat dinner?"

"Do boys think about only that one thing all the time?" After a small pause I continue, "And by the way, that's not your gift."

But quickly I correct myself to avoid any argument, "I mean . . . it could be . . . but there is something else . . . keep guessing," I say, unwrapping myself from his arm.

"I am starving, let's eat first and then talk."

*****

He enjoys every bit of food. Taking a bite, he says, "Yum . . . malai kofta . . . so soft. It is melting in my mouth like . . . uummm," he eats the sentence with a bite of kofta. This much praise from him, I can't believe. He appears as a different person than a regular him. But I am glad he enjoys the food.

After dinner, when I wash my hands in the bathroom sink, he comes behind me. He slides his hands to the sink tap from under my hands, with his elbows touching my waist. Without moving his gaze from me for even a fraction of a second, he picks me up and takes me to the bedroom.

"So, what is my gift?" he asks while dropping me gently on the bed.

"OK, I will tell you everything regarding the special gift," I agree getting down on the bed. I move close to him. I curl myself in his arms and he snuggles me tight putting his hands around me.

"You know what, I am extremely happy. Once you find out, you will be super glad too."

"And, what is it?" he asks impatiently this time, like a kid.

"We are going to have a baby," I say. And all of a sudden his arms that wrapped me tightly before, loosen instead of going tauter, contradictory to my anticipation.

"No way, you are pregnant."

"Yes, I am."

Taking his arms completely off me, he asks, as if to force his opinion on me, "Don't you think it's too early to have a baby? We have been married only for a year now. I am not ready yet." He thumps on the bed looking upset, profoundly thinking about something.

I anticipated a different reaction. I expected, as soon as he would know, he would pick me up. Perhaps, he would jump like kids to reveal his joy. He would kiss my forehead and would like to touch my tummy to connect with the baby. But again, I can never predict how he reacts at any given time. Spending life with him is like always walking on eggshells.

"But, I am ready. Anyways, I can't work because of visa issues. This is the perfect time to have a baby. When you are at work for hours together, I feel lonely. Baby will keep me busy." I put my side of the coin on the table.

When he doesn't buy it, I continue, "Since I came to know, I have been talking to baby a lot. I already feel connected with it. I feel as if this baby has already become an integral part of our lives."

Sitting next to him on the bed, holding his hand I tell him he is unable to envision the joy that baby will bring in our world.

"Trust me, you will be happy to hold the baby in your arms."

Then I stand facing him (he is sitting on the bed and I am standing). Looking into his eyes, I assure him, "You know when baby will call us dada and mama first time, we will love it. We will dance for sure. We will cry tears of joy."

Expressing that thought brings a smile to my eyes; but his eyes do not display the same. He doesn't respond at all. He is awfully quiet, which is terrifying. One second's silence turns to one minute to one hour.

Finally, I plead, looking at him, "Please, Rajeev, say something."

I have never seen him like this before. He is never this quiet. He is always either talking or screaming. This is different. I feel weary, weary of pleading with him to speak, weary of wondering what will happen next.

"I am tired. I think we should get some rest now. We will talk on this tomorrow," I call out finally. Most of the night, we both cannot sleep peacefully.

I don't know when I go into a sound sleep. I wake up with the sound of the door closing. When I get up, I don't see him around. I figure he must have left for the office. Clock shows 6:30 AM. It is still early for him to leave home.

Maybe he needs time to digest the news; I come up with a self-made excuse to make peace with the questions running in my mind relating to his silence.

Shall I talk to my parents or his parents? I contemplate.

But I prefer waiting till we talk one more time before speaking to our parents.

My day starts with morning sickness, which continues the whole day on and off. In spite of the queasiness and Rajeev's silence, I very much love the precious feeling of a new life shaping within me. I feel no less than marvelous. In my head, I compile a list of some names for a girl and a few for a boy. I imagine me touching baby's soft toes and kissing baby's cute little hands. I visualize pulling baby's googly woogly, soft and squishy cheeks. I plan on buying loads of cute little clothes and soft toys for my little angel. But all this is possible only if Rajeev is equally happy.

*****

When I hear the door opening, I glance at the clock. It is Rajeev. He has come home at 3:00 PM, way earlier than his routine time to be back from the office. In the last year, he has hardly ever returned from the office this early. I come out of our bedroom and hug him. He still appears upset. He sits on the sofa without saying much. Finally, when he talks, I sense that the worst time of my life is chasing me.

"How could you even think about that?" I scream. I have never raised my voice this high. I shiver and tremble from my own screeching sound. Or perhaps from the scary thought of what he said. I don't want to kill my unborn. I want my baby to grow up in front of me, be a happy, sensible individual unlike his father and one day stand up against his dad for me, for himself and for the right things in life.

"It is our baby. I cannot kill my baby," I cry it out. I pity his thoughts. He thinks a baby will bring an end to his career and an end to his married life. He wants to attain a certain level in his career before he plans on a baby. As usual, he only thinks about himself and about what he wants. Every decision revolves around his own needs and wants. Hours and hours of weeping and sobbing don't melt his heart as if he has a heart of stone.

"I don't want to abort our baby. If we do so, we will regret it later in our life. Let's continue with this pregnancy. I promise, I will never ask for anything more in life." I try every option possible to persuade him to not to take away the life of our unborn baby.

Nothing changes his decision. I don't realize, one more time in my life, how I turn submissive to somebody else's wish, in spite of it being not only contradictory to mine, but also wrong to an unbelievable extent. Even though I am completely shaken by his decision, I give up in two days. The house is full of dreaded silence and the hatred. This environment is not what I want for my baby. A little did I understand then, that standing up for myself might have done some good.

He wants to share our decision with his parents— only his parents and not my parents. The reason, I am told, is that his mom is a doctor, and she should know if either one of us is undergoing any medical procedure. But I know the unsaid; he is so close to his mom that in future, he wouldn't like to get the blame of not sharing a big decision with her. He calls his parents, keeping the phone on speaker mode and narrates the entire situation. His mom gets emotional hearing about a grandchild. She would convince her son, I think in my mind, raising my hopes. Thankful, for the first time in the whole last year, for the bond this mom-son duo shares.

But all in vain. After around forty-five minutes of conversation, when my mom-in-law cannot convince her son, she plays a smart chess move that gives me brain freeze; not knowing how to move ahead, she replaces herself with me. Now I have to continue her chess game against her son. But no matter which next move I take in the game, I will be the one who loses.

My father-in-law is silent throughout the call as if he knows what will happen next. As if from the years of experience, he already discerns either son wins or his mom. She wants to talk to me only. Rajeev passes the phone to me after taking it out of speaker mode. She then states bluntly, "Sonia, if you abort the baby I will never ever talk to you in my life and I mean it. Now figure this out."

I have always made everyone around me happy at my cost. I don't see anything different happening this time either. The words of my mom-in-law echo in my ears. I am frightened by what she says and how she says it. If his mom could not convince him, there is no way I can persuade him. Not that I haven't tried for the last two days.

The kind of emotional pressure, I am going under, it is unbearable. In my mind, I pray to God for this difficult time to pass soon. I pray for the almighty to make a decision in my favor. But He also helps only those who help themselves. I decide to not approve of Rajeev's decision.

When I sway from my agreement to his decision of abortion, he fumes in anger and doesn't even refrain from hitting me. The little bit of courage that I have gathered to oppose the homicide of my own baby, is crumbled and crushed like a piece of paper. When he thrusts me against the door, slaps me and pulls my hair, I don't stand up for myself anymore to stop him from beating me. And in turn I don't halt him from murdering my baby.

Instead of asking for help from my family sitting faraway on the other side of the world or from our friendly neighbors, I silently give in. I am scared to ask for help from my parents or even share this with them. I don't want to ruin their life with my tensions. They already had enough from me during college days.

*****

Two weeks later

On a gloomy afternoon, one life is erased. The stomach cramps and physical pain that I go through seem minuscule compared to my heartache. Tears roll down from my heart. My mind is disturbed. I blame myself for whatever happened. One year ago, I took a big step to rejuvenate my life by marrying a guy. And here I revitalize my life by killing an unborn baby. I regret my choice to marry him. I feel nothing but remorse for all the decisions of my life so far. I repent once again for not standing up for myself. All these thoughts make me emotionally weaker. A relationship with sadness is not new to me by now. But this time around, the depth of it is beyond anything I ever witnessed or even imagined.

After the abortion, he stands by my side. But I feel disgusted to be by him. The way he changes his mood and behavior rapidly, I am aghast. The same person didn't even want to talk to me for a few days, in spite of me weeping continuously. Now he comes to embrace me. I can't stand him. I am also ashamed of myself that for such a narrow-minded, selfish, and unkind man, I let my child be slain.

Our relationship is going through one awkward phase of life. I feel vulnerable. I can't talk to anyone about the emotional trauma that I go through. He thinks it is not a big deal to abort a baby. But for me it is. I sense the intensity of emotional pain more than the actual physical pain. I regret my compliance. My mom-in-law, who knows about it, is already enraged. I don't want to share this with my mom knowing what her reaction will be. I am in a part of the world with no close friends around. Once again I find myself in a phase of life where I have been before a few years back, all alone. I have no one. Hour by hour, I get more and more susceptible. I want to go back to Esha. I badly miss her. The temptation to go to her wears me thin. My marriage with Rajeev has filled my life with emptiness. I was hopeful to wipe out that emptiness with the love and giggles of a little one. But that hope has left me hollow double fold now.

*****

After one week
Sunday mid-morning
Rajeev asks me to get ready to go out. To my surprise, he takes me to the New York-New Jersey Art Fairs and Craft Show.

He mentions before leaving, "Lately, you look miserable and unhappy. I thought I should take you out on a treat you would like."

How wouldn't I feel miserable after murdering our baby, I think but don't say it. I loathe the care that he shows to cover his brutal and inhuman act.

Then he continues, "The place, where I am taking you, has an exhibition of artwork of talented artists like you. You would get to see nice paintings too."

I am not excited that I will get to see the nice paintings. What he does to cheer me up, nothing matters anymore.

After the abortion, each minute, mentally I go away and away from him. I strongly desire to run away. But in this part of the world, with dependent visa limitations, I have no choice. I want to live my life in my own way on my terms going forward. I repent that I should have continued my pregnancy by myself. But by the time I get the urge to do so, it is already too late. There is no point in having that desire now.

*****

I force myself to pay attention to the craft show just to avoid Rajeev and his so-called care. Slowly, the fabulous artworks have a magnetic effect on me. I am overwhelmed by the sight of the art pieces and splendid work done by many. There is so much talent around the world that is still hidden, I believe. The traffic of people flows from every direction to see the wonderful artistries. Knowing the journey of many artists to get to the place where they are today gives me goose bumps. Secretly, I wish to be one of them, exhibiting my own paintings, someday. I also want Esha by my side during those exhibitions. I think about her. I wonder if she still paints. I assume her passion for painting must have driven her to take it as a career.

As we enter the first lane of the exhibition, on the right-hand side I see a few food stalls. The smell of popcorn mingled with elephant ears plus French fries attracts people to buy this munchies. A few high-school-age-kids are selling lemonade. They enjoy each other's company more than selling anything. They are accompanied by two adults. I am not sure if they are teachers or parents of those kids. The banner near a tent mentions the fundraising they are doing is for Children's Cancer Hospital of the area. I immediately run to the stall and buy two lemonade bottles using a five dollar bill that I saved during my last grocery trip.

After passing the food stalls, we enter the area where the first few tents sell handmade accessories like leather purses, bead necklaces, earrings, bracelets, cotton bags and large ceramic pots. Every piece is skillfully made. No design and pattern of any single leather purse is repeated. Each ceramic pot has a different shape and a beautiful carving. At the end of this first lane, many wooden benches and stools are presented for sale. All handmade. Exquisite! For a second, I wish I had a lot of money to buy everything I like.

From here on, the crowd turns to the right lane to enter the area I am most interested in. I go inside the first tent. It displays abstract painting art. I am stunned to look at them. Each painting is given a unique and suitable name by the artist. I go through a couple of tents. For the time being, I forget about the pain I am fighting. The guilt that I feel for being equally responsible for the murder of my baby dissolves in the colors and emotions of those paintings.

The fifth tent on my right-hand side is overcrowded. We can't even step in. We can only see a few portraits displayed outside of the tent. I am impressed and in love with those that I want to go inside to see more. Somehow, it reminds me of Esha. Rajeev doesn't want to go in to avoid the crowd. But I turn into a stubborn kid who cries for ice cream. Finally he agrees. I instantly notice I didn't give up on something I really wanted.

After waiting for half an hour in a queue, we get to go inside the tent to look at all the work. That half an hour wait was the most worthwhile of all when I see the person behind those wonderful paintings. As soon as I see her, I cling to her and cry. Everybody around us at first tries to call security to get me away. They think I am troubling the artist. But soon they realize that we are friends. The noise of the surrounding crowd suddenly turns into a pin drop silence. All the eyes poke me through that quietness. I let go of my arm wrap, which was holding her tight. Then I introduce Esha to Rajeev. Without taking much of her time, we exchange numbers. Rajeev insists on her to call me because I have no other friends here yet. She also promises to come to our home once this exhibition ends.

CHAPTER 21. MIRACLES DO HAPPEN

June 2012
First Thursday of the month

RAJEEV LEAVES FOR THE OFFICE. I fix the living room and then take a shower. I want to be all ready before Esha arrives. During exhibition week once on her way home she called me. Since Rajeev was around I couldn't talk to her much. She mentioned that she can only come on Thursday because her painting gallery is closed that day and Saturday. But her kids are home with her on Saturday while other days they go to day care. Moreover Rajeev could be home on Saturday. He being around may make our meeting awkward and tricky. So I pick Thursday.

I can't wait to see her. I also can't contain my excitement to hear all about her gallery. I am glad that her dream of having her own painting gallery has come true. I also have all the questions for her as burning as many years back when she left me. But the happy feeling of meeting her is dominant over those questions. Maybe this is God's sign for us to be together again. My hopes fly high one more time even without talking to her. The feeling of intuition is strong.

She still looks gorgeous as she always did, eight years back. I love the orange color A-line silhouette dress on her that stops just above her knees. She still looks fresh and full of energy as always. Who would believe this girl is the mother of two tots?

"You look fabulous," I say, hugging her.

Landing a peck on my cheek, she retorts, "You look stunning in this pencil skirt and body-hugging top. That's a new style for my girl."

The way she kisses me and calls me "my girl" drives me crazy one more time for her, all over again. I can't believe how much I have missed her. Her eyes are still as easy-to-read as ever. I can recognize longing in her eyes, longing for love, longing for me. But I am scared of that. I won't be able to handle it if she leaves me one more time. So I hold my racing heart and step back. Apart from desire, I also see pain in her eyes. The pain that may have taken away gleam from her eyes. The pain that she may not have shared with anyone. Perhaps today she may spill that sting out in my company.

Suddenly, she mentions about what and how she felt after seeing me in the mall that recent Sunday afternoon and how remorseful she was for not talking to me that day.

She says, "All the way to home, I kept cursing myself under my breath for not speaking to you, for not taking your number and for losing that one more chance to be with you."

Oh wow . . . she also wants to be with me, I say to myself, with a bit of excitement. Immediately another thought follows. *But why? Is she not happy in her marriage? What about her kids?* I force myself not to think anything, but just listen to her.

She continues, "After seeing you, for a few days, I couldn't think of anything else, but you. That is when I decided I would go to the mall again in the hope to see you, in the hope to find you once more."

"Ah," I mutter.

She doesn't stop. "I was becoming fussy thinking about you, more and more with every passing hour. I have never been grouchy to that extent in the last eight years in spite of my troubled and ready for divorce marriage. Not that I care about the cheater husband of mine anymore, but still . . ."

Then she adds that she went to the mall on Sunday at the exact same time when she saw me there. She did it for a few Sundays leaving her kids with her husband.

One Sunday when she went there, she left kids with her husband at home again. She kept waiting near the kids play area in an urge to see me. Somehow she believed I would be there around that time. After one and a half hours of waiting, she walked nervously to and fro between the kids play area and a nearby Gap store. Whenever she saw any girl coming toward the play area, she prayed and begged, "God, please bring her here. Please God!" After walking around a few times, she went inside the kids area, sat down on a bench, with her purse in her lap, her body leaning into it, tears falling on the cell phone holder pocket. To her disappointment, I did not appear, yet she was not ready to accept that she might not see me again in her life. Esha wiped her own tears, attending to the call from her husband. He called her to let her know how hard Harsh was crying for his mom. Esha could barely hear him on the phone, all she heard was her son's cry. He was screaming and crying to death, "Not you Dadda, I want my mommaaaaaaaaaaaaa . . . waa . . . waa."

How kids take priority over everything! She left immediately to go back to her kids, in spite of her unwillingness. But this tough girl was determined to come back to the mall again, next Sunday, then the following Sunday and every damn Sunday till she found me.

As soon as she finishes, in an impulse I hug her tight and cry it out, "I missed you too Esha. I love you."

The spark kindles again. She pours all her love out on me once more. She longed for me as much as I did, maybe even more. I go close to hug her, but she brings her lips close to mine. This time the intensity with which she holds, kisses, and loves me, guarantees me that this togetherness is forever now, no matter what.

I share with her highlights of those years of my life after she left. She is sorry that she left me. After a little while, I offer her tea and we both walk to the kitchen to make tea together. That is when she shares her side of our past.

When she was in second year engineering, her dad had a heart attack from thinking too much about the unfortunate trip incident. Fortunately, he was saved. During her final year, he had another massive heart attack. The doctors said he could die any time. So, before he passed away, he wanted her to marry a suitable guy of his choice. She got married just for him. A month after her wedding, her dad died. Since then her mom visits her here every year and stays with her for 5–6 months to spend time with the kids. It's her mom who found out about her husband's extramarital affair last year. Esha had always been a devoted mother who literally was oblivious of the many wrong things that were even happening to her and around her. Later it became open knowledge that her husband's affair had been going for years, even before their marriage. His parents wouldn't agree to him marrying a Spanish girl. At last he married Esha to make his parents happy and to cover up his love affair.

I can't imagine how Esha might have felt when she found out him cheating on her and that too after having two kids and many years in their marriage. Last year when she found it out, she filed for a divorce and he was ready for it so that he could marry his girlfriend. Her divorce could happen any time now, maybe in two weeks.

*****

She is pleased to know that Di and I share the best relationship now. I tell her about the forced abortion I went through a few weeks back. I cannot hold myself back; tears bubble in my eyes. I sob loudly. Holding me tight, her eyes turn watery too. She moans along with me. The pang of the abortion feels less with her being by my side. I wish to spend the rest of my life with her. But I don't know yet how it would be possible if at all.

She pleads for forgiveness one more time for she left me to fulfill her dad's promise. She considers her act of leaving me as her dishonesty toward our relationship. For her dishonesty, she thinks, God punished her in his own way that she never was loved by her husband. But according to me, her husband cheating on her and my husband forcing me to abort the child was all done by God to carve the path for us to meet each other once again. Maybe this is the chance for us to be together this time around.

I politely express, "I forgave you when Girish gave me your message. I loved you before, I still love you and will always do."

After hours of heart to heart conversation, we breathe a sigh of delight as if everything will be OK now since we have got each other again. After filling our hearts by catching up on many years, to satiate our growling stomachs, we make sandwiches.

Putting our endless talk on pause, Esha leaves to pick up her kids from day care with a promise to come back following Thursday again.

*****

Tuesday
I work on a painting that I started yesterday. In the last year, I sometimes worked on my hobby but not a lot. After meeting Esha again, I am delighted and want to paint something beautiful.

Suddenly, I leave the painting halfway. Get ready in a jiffy to go to her gallery. Rummage through my purse for a visiting card of Esha's painting gallery. She gave me the card before leaving, on the day when she came to my apartment. I was overjoyed seeing her, I didn't even bother to look at the card. I grab the card and turn on the computer to find the directions to her gallery from my place. When I look at the card again to confirm the address that I type, the name of her gallery takes me by surprise.

"Wow, she really missed me. This name is the proof that she loves me dearly," I whisper to myself.

I am glad she never banished me from her heart, no matter even if she left me for whatever reasons. For these many years, I always thought her grip on my heart is robust and forever. But oh boy . . . my grip on her heart is equally strong too. I am ecstatic. The world feels like a whimsical place once more. The sight of sadness is vanishing. I see it walking out of me. I feel happiness rising in my throat and my eyes making way for joyful tears to roll out. I am sure my lonely days will fade soon. This time, I have to take control of what I want. No more being submissive, is my determination.

Printing the directions to her gallery and jotting down all the bus numbers—the buses that I have to catch to reach her gallery—I leave. I am a little nervous to go that far by myself without having any knowledge about bus service of the area. I have to change three buses to reach to her. I have gone to the supermarket near our apartment many times by myself. Only one bus though. But I am sure I can do this; anything to see her. Love brings out all the positive forces of one together to do what one wants to accomplish.

I drop by her gallery as a surprise. I want to see her expressions, the delight on her face, when she least expects me.

Rajeev is absolutely unaware of our—Esha and my—relationship. I don't feel guilty to hide it from him. I don't feel guilty to leave the person who forced me to kill our own baby. I don't feel guilty to leave the person who is abusive. Now, I will not shy away from breaking norms. I am disgusted to go even close to him. I will tell him everything when the appropriate time arrives that is after my visa issues are resolved.

"Sweetie, what a pleasant surprise," she says with gleaming eyes and a sweet smile as soon as she sees me entering.

She comes running to me. And with a glow in my eyes, I thank her, "Thanks for always keeping me in your heart. The name Sonisha for your gallery, says it all."

Then she hugs me like never before. I want to seize this moment of happiness forever. But, does one really have control over the time? No, I guess; for the next instant comes following to grab the previous one when a couple enters to the shop. I look around at paintings while she attends her customers. I am so proud of her and her work. The hard work, effort, and time to set up this place must have been massive. This results from the power of her passion. A passion that releases nothing but positive energy within one to overcome the roadblocks to the goal and thereafter.

Once the customers leave, she tells me about her journey to this beautiful destination of her dream, of her passion. It's amazing to know how Laksh (one student who also went to painting class with us) and Kabir sir helped Esha to set up this gallery, especially Laksh with his contacts around New York. He himself comes to exhibit his paintings here at least once every six months. He owns two galleries in Mumbai. In a moment, I fly to dream land. I envision the dream of Esha and me painting together as a team, the best team of the two ever as we used to be during Kabir sir's classes. Then a smile gently touches my face, leaving Esha with a big question relating to it.

I share with Esha the thought that brought a smile on my face. I accept out loud my whim to be with her forever and also be a part of a painting team with her as old times. She heartily chuckles, and then as she speaks her voice trembles from tears that are choking her throat.

"It can't be coincidence," she says with a quivering but relieved voice. "Since this past Thursday when I met you, I have been urging for the same too. In fact I have already laid out a plan in my head." Then she shares her plan for the two of us to be together. She has figured it out, how and when to proceed further. In her head, she has listed the issues that we might face to come together. She continues to work on finding the resolution for those problems with the help of her lawyer. We both discuss it out.

Financially, she can support me if I leave Rajeev right away. She lives in an apartment, not with her husband anymore. She left his house last year when she came to know about his lifelong affair. She is independent enough to take care of her family and me as well. Moreover, I will join her work once we live together.

The only thing we are worried about is my visa status. Officially, same-sex marriage is not legal yet. But it will be legal pretty soon, she mentions. So I can't get any visa or permanent residency by moving in with her right now. Then she declares that she will talk to her lawyer. She promises to grapple with the matter herself.

The idea of we two being together captivates us and we wish to conquer all the obstacles. It gives me a new ray of sunshine.

She gives me a tour of her gallery. I truly enjoy seeing her paintings and being in her company. As always her work shows her great vim, but most of the paintings have a kind of ache hidden in them; my heart could notice those minute details in her work. Of all, one painting catches my eyes, mind, and the attention. It feels so true, the unique idea of all. It is a simple but powerful painting. It says a lot about our relationship.

Marriage (painted in green with beautiful leaves around it) and Hearts (painted in red).

Marriage = ❤ + ❤

Then I request her to keep this painting aside for our house instead of selling it. How couldn't she agree?

*****

As per the plan, Thursday when Esha comes to my apartment again, she takes me out for lunch. Rain settles on the town for the entire day. Flowers bloom. It feels like a cue to us. Our life will blossom exactly like these flowers. Leaving this beautiful day outside, we enter a cold, dark room that keeps the secret of many lovers. Sitting in the dark, holding each other's hand, we enjoy a movie together after almost eight years. Things feel different in her company. This cinema theater is not just a dark, cold room with a few chairs and a wall showing the projection of a reel. Rather it is a place to remember forever. To remember how we held each other's hand with no fear, how we whispered sweet nothings in each other's ears and how we promised each other to be together forever. I feel as if I have come to visit my own dream. The dream that I never want to end. We make good memories once again. This time around to last forever.

Her presence makes everything worth it. Love makes me see things differently. In her presence, I forget the past. I forget that she left me. I forget that a life inside me was killed. All I feel is, there can't be any other moment than this. There will be no better or worse, bigger or smaller moment than this. This is it. She is with me. That is all that matters.

*****

I miss Di and Girish both. I want to share the news with them, but again I don't want to take any risks in this matter. It might reach to my parents somehow or to Rajeev and everything would be ruined. The risk in love is loss. I can't afford that risk one more time in my life.

After many years, the first time when I saw Esha in the mall, her eyes looked vapid and soft with sorrow. But those eyes are regaining their twinkle. Spending time in each other's company makes us happier every second. It seems the weeks are passing at a snail's pace. I can't live with her until her divorce is done. She is afraid that if her husband finds out about our relationship, he may use it in his favor to get full custody of the kids.

I want to meet her kids. Our plan of me spending time with them works perfectly fine as if God, himself, is holding our hands and making us move according to his master plot. Due to a heavy workload and project deadlines coming closer, Rajeev goes to the office on Saturday, instantly I leave for her house. Before I move in with them, we want her kids to know me, and feel comfortable being around me. Esha preps them well by sharing fun stories of us. She shares our painting class partnership stories. She also tells them how incredibly well we both worked as a team. Esha mentions that they are excited about my visit. Her kids make greeting cards to welcome me. They are both happy to see me since they hardly have any visitors here in the USA, except their grandma.

Harsh and Gauri give me a tight and big hug like their mom taught them. They both hand over the cards they made. "What a warm gesture! That is sweet of you kiddos," I say, looking at the cards and sitting down on the sofa between both of them. Then I continue, "Because you both are irresistibly sweet, here is something for you." I fish out their gifts from the gift bag. I made a pit stop at a mall before going to their place. I see a gleam in Harsh's eye when he sees a Thomas the Tank Engine toy. I came to know from Esha regarding his newborn craze for this train. Nowadays, he watches, reads, and plays Thomas the Tank Engine only. Gauri loves to play with Barbie dolls. So she is on cloud nine holding the mermaid Barbie I have brought for her.

"Aunt Soni, how did you know I wanted this?" she inquires with curious eyes.

"This aunt knows magic. She knows everything," I reply playfully and tickle her. The awe on her face leaves me amazed. It surprises me how easily kids get amused by the explanation of certain things they get from adults.

Little Harsh and I become buddies. At first, he loves to play peek-a-boo with me. After a while, he wants to play hide-n-seek. When hiding, he takes his Thomas train to hide it too. Doll Gauri can't stop singing her rhymes for me. She enjoys being the center of attention and loves receiving the praise relating to how well she sings and how cute she looks. She is an exact copy of Esha as I thought when I first saw her in the mall.

When it is time for me to go back home before Rajeev arrives, they both cry and don't want me to leave. With a promise that I will be back soon to live with them forever, they let me go.

Esha's lawyer recommends me not to leave Rajeev to move in with her till either our—Rajeev and my—green card arrives or we—Esha and I—plan to move back to India permanently. We choose the first option. That means we have to wait till I get my U.S. permanent residency. But he also mentions that you may get it soon since your application date of 2005 has become current now. Every passing day, it becomes tougher to live without her.

*****

July 2010

A few weeks pass by. But the uncontrollable and unstoppable desire to live with Esha doesn't let me focus on anything. Sometimes I think it is amazing how love acts like an addictive drug and always keeps one high.

Esha's divorce is finally done. I am still stuck because of my immigration status. Rajeev is getting excited about going on our cruise vacation coming in two weeks. I don't want to go with him at all now. Not talking to Esha and her kids while on the cruise will be difficult. Now her kids chat with me every day. After coming home from day care, they talk to me first and then carry on with their routine. I always chat with them before Rajeev reaches home.

Day by day, I turn into an impatient green card seeker immigrant. I am as impatient as a child on Christmas Eve. I wait for Santa every day in the hope to receive my Christmas gift now.

Finally, after one week, my wish is granted. My Christmas gift—our green card—arrives five months before the real Christmas Eve.

Everything is falling into place; otherwise it can't be coincidental that same-sex marriage becomes legal in the U.S. state of New York effective the same day as the arrival of my green card. When I see it in our mail box, I first call Esha and we figure out our plan for the coming Thursday.

I sit down to write a long letter to Rajeev. I want to leave him the letter when I go to Esha's house. I want to jot down everything that I never shared with him before. But I don't know why, my hands shiver. I can't pen a single word. As strange as it may sound, it feels as if I am stabbing him in the back. Abruptly, the promise of not leaving your husband until death hits me hard. I feel as if I am a demon who doesn't want to play by the rules of marriage. In spite of all his mistakes, it feels like I am doing something wrong, something immoral. I drop the pen on the table and cry out loud.

Later that evening, Esha leaves her gallery early. Before picking up the kids, she stops by my place for a surprise visit to celebrate completion of my green card process. She brings a black forest cake and a nice greeting card. I see the feeling of pure joy in her eyes. But I don't know why, I am unable to share that joy. Suddenly, the thought of breaking the marriage vows for an aspired love, seems selfish to me.

Just as she is leaving to go, Rajeev comes home. With a surprised look, he greets her. Immediately, she leaves, explaining that it is time to pick up her kids.

"You never mentioned she visits often," he says as soon as she has left.

"No, she doesn't," I fumble from the shock of seeing him home early. I didn't expect him that early.

He demands a cup of tea. I put water and tea powder together for boiling on the stove in a small pot.

Suddenly, I hear a noise. Instantly, I whirl around to see the remote control lying broken near the window right next to the TV. Rajeev walks toward the kitchen. He looks furious. All of a sudden, I notice the card that Esha gave me a few minutes back in his hand.

"Oh, shit." In the hassle of her leaving and him entering at the same time, I forgot to hide it.

Even before I can move away from the kitchen, he comes close to me, his eye oozing anger and fury. Holding my hair in one hand, he pushes my head to hit against the wall. I try to stop him, but he seems so much stronger while in anger.

I am scared of him more than before when I see blood oozing from my forehead. I cannot move. I feel dizzy. He sits down near me. He reads the card out loud in a mean way. Then he jumps up screaming, "How the hell can she call you my love?"

Unexpectedly, he takes a pot from the stove. I could smell the pot burning. The tea water might have evaporated already. He places that hot pot on my left calf leaving me burned. What happened after that I don't remember!

When I open my eyes, I am lying on the bed. He is sitting by me, still agitated, but putting ointment on the burned area of my leg. I can never decipher his way of handling any matter. He first abuses me giving scars that will last a lifetime and then he puts on medicine to sooth them. I am still scared, but I don't say a word; my hands are shaky. I try to look in his eyes for consolation. But all I see there is a flat smirk.

"Tell me everything that is going on between you two. I will not hurt you, I promise," he consoles me.

I am still scared inside out. My heart pumps faster.

"Tell me," he demands loudly. "I want to know," comes a softer follow up.

"Nothing has happened. We went to the same school before. Just friends I promise," I blurt out in fright, my lips trembling.

"Please do not hit me," I stammer.

Finally, night falls on us. Rajeev is in deep sleep. I cry frantically with my mouth shut, so he does not hear me. I am crouched in a fetal position, with a blanket stuffed in my hands. I cannot bear the pain. I do not remember when I fall asleep.

The next day when I wake up I see he is home. I am still frightened but I gather myself together to make tea for him. I can't walk easily because of the pain from the burned area of my calf. I limp heavily and it feels as if I won't be able to get as far as the kitchen. But somehow I manage to reach there. He is still quiet, a stern look on his face. Suddenly our phone rings. He picks it up.

"I told you something urgent has come up, I cannot leave home," Rajeev screams into the phone.

After a pause, he says, "OK, but only for fifteen minutes that is it. I know. I know . . . the world will fall if I do not show up. I have heard it many times now. OK, I will be there for fifteen minutes only, but after that I will have to leave. OK?"

He hangs up. "I will be back soon. Hope you feel better by then," prompts Rajeev.

As soon as he steps out, I call Esha and inform her on what he did.

Without giving a second thought, she says, "I will come and get you right now while he is at work."

"The physical and emotional pain and wounds that Rajeev has given you in the last year are forever. Only time will heal them. But if you continue to stay with him even for one extra day, his brutal acts will not stop." This is what Esha iterates a few times over the phone before hanging up. And I agree with her.

Before Esha arrives to pick me up, I finally write to Rajeev, telling him everything that I always wanted to say but didn't have enough courage. I jot down about my relationship with Esha, about the hurt that still resides in me from all his verbal, physical, and sexual abuse. And the most excruciating of all, the cruel act of killing our baby that he forced me into.

I ask him not to try to find me. I also mention to him that by the time he would see this letter my parents would already know about it too.

I walk out of the house leaving everything behind. Drowning my fears and parting from the whole shebang—material things, imbued with much everlasting pain that he gave me in this house, I go with her.

Esha first takes me to a doctor. Immediately following, we visit her Lawyer to file for my divorce. It feels as if everything is being taken care of by her.

In a few days, the lawyer delivers the divorce papers to Rajeev.

For the first few days I worry, what if he finds me, what if he beats me again, but then I convince myself to put that side of my life to rest.

I share the news—of me now staying with Esha— with Di, Jiju, and Girish in the order as written. This leaves them numb at first. Slowly absorbing the fact and after knowing how and why I did it, they all warmly approve of this relationship as I predicted. But my parents are heated at me and have not talked to me for seven days now. I would have been contented if they too would have given their approvals to us. Esha's mom is cool about we two being together. Nevertheless, we two have been excellent companions always and her mom also knows about the betrayal with which her daughter was treated.

*****

A few weeks later, I prepare breakfast for Gauri and Harsh and then drop them off at school. When I come back, Esha is still home. I am surprised to see her.

"Esha, you have not gone yet. Is everything all right?" I ask. Then I notice she is wearing a pretty, silver color sleeveless, glittery dress. She looks stunningly gorgeous, but the outfit surely seems odd for this time of the day.

"Esha, is everything OK?" I ask with concern.

Then I see it happening. She comes close, bends down on one knee and holds my hands in hers. I am shocked and happy.

"Esha!" I utter.

She looks straight in my eyes and says,

"Life is love. Love is you."

"Soni, I love you from bottom of my heart and promise to do anything to make you happy."

"I can't imagine another day of my life without you. I promise to be by you till the end."

"The world seems a magical place whenever I think about you, dream about you. Would you like to make my world even more magical? Will you marry me?"

A few seconds of silence . . .

I go breathless and then utter a cry of joy, "Yes, I will."

EPILOGUE

Sonia and Rajeev's divorce goes through smoothly.

Sonia and Esha got engaged in a private small celebration.

They had a big, lavish, bang on wedding within six months after they lived together.

At first Sonia's parents didn't talk to her for few months. Di, Jiju, and Girish helped turn them around. Sonia's parents showered their blessings on their daughter on her wedding, for which they went to the USA.

Girish, a well-known cardiologist of Mumbai now, is happily married to his college-time doctor girlfriend. They enjoy serving people for the well-being of their heart and life. Not to mention, both of them are minting money.

Di, Jiju, and their kiddo are a happy family too. Di's daughter is a bright and wonderful child. She has got the beauty of her mom and the brains of her dad, the perfect combo.

Abhay found his soulmate and is happily married to her. He is still friends with Sonia. He and his wife recently visited Sonisha when they went to New York for a conference.

Sonia and Esha's career life is at the peak and so is their family life. They both started one more painting gallery in another part of the town and called it "Soul Mates." They are now the owners of a cozy house in New Jersey.

Sonia and Esha are now an active part of Madadgar virtual team. They both find immense pleasure in supporting others through this group.

The kids are growing fast. Gauri and Harsh love Sonia as much as they love Esha.

Now when Gauri goes to her school, she tells her friends she has two moms. She increasingly loves Sonia every day as a part of her life. Harsh likes Sonia so much that he is always picky about getting only her help over Esha's. They are a nice little family, which is getting bigger now. They are preparing to welcome one more family member. Yes, Sonia will have a baby soon, the blessing of advanced medical science.

MUSIC LOVE

'Where words leave off, music begins', said German poet and journalist Heinrich Heine of the 19th century.

He said it rightly. Many times in our life, when we fall short of words, music plays the most significant role. When in love, we experience it the most. So did the characters of this book.

I am grateful to those artists who add spirit to our soul, joy to our hearts and dance to our feet with their music.

Baby, baby, can't you hear my heartbeat?: by Herman's Hermits Band from 1960's

Love is All Around: originally recorded by English rock band The Troggs. But the version that inspired me to pick this song is by a Scottish band Wet Wet Wet

And I Love Her: by The Beatles

ACKNOWLEDGEMENTS

This book is a result of hard work and contribution of many individuals. Everyday life moments have played some or other role in making of this story. If I were to write each one of those contributors, I would run out of space. But there are few who just have to be mentioned as they played a big role in my book making journey.

A huge thank you to my parents who encouraged me to write when I shared my desire to write a novel. A special thank you to my mom for keeping check on percent completion of book from time to time. That brought me on writing track from distracted everyday tasks. A big thank you to my father-in-law who tirelessly took care of kids when I sat in my office room or at Starbucks for long hours to finish the editing of the book.

To my husband, Bhushan, who has been involved in the book since the first draft. Thank you so much for your constant support and critique in shaping this book. This book is as much yours as it is mine. I couldn't have done it without you. I am fortunate to have found you as my life partner. To my adorable kids, Bhumika and Neel – who left me alone in my room to write whenever I said mommy needed to write. I love you both; you make my world even more beautiful. Your smile, hugs and kisses are the biggest stress buster of my life.

To Aneetha R. – my soul sister, one of my closest friends, thank you for always being there to encourage me to write. Thank you so much for the endless feedback on every matter related to this book. I am lucky to have you my sister. To AJ Powell and Taran J. – thank you for taking time and reading the first raw draft of my manuscript. This book wouldn't have been possible without your honest feedback and encouragement.

To my talented illustrator Tasneem A. – thank you for creating beautiful book cover.

To Adarsha D. – my creative head – thank you for finding me great illustrator, animators and production house. A big thank you for coordinating all the work related to book video teaser. To Sumeet M. – thank you for creating captivating book video teaser.

To all other family and friends – thank you for believing in me, encouraging me to write. Thank you all for your kind words and reinforcement.

A NOTE FROM MITA BALANI

Thank you so much for reading Breaking Norms. If you enjoyed it, please take a moment to leave a review at your favorite online retailer such as Amazon USA or Amazon India.

I welcome contact from readers. At my website, you can contact me, sign up for my newsletter to be notified of new releases, read my blog, and find me on social media.

http://www.MitaBalani.com

-Mita Balani

Made in United States
Troutdale, OR
09/29/2023